Queen City Corpse

A Sebastian McCabe – Jeff Cody Mystery

Dan Andriacco

First edition published in 2017
© Copyright 2017
Dan Andriacco

Paperback ISBN 978-1-78705-141-6
ePub ISBN 978-1-78705-142-3
PDF ISBN 978-1-78705-143-0

Published in the UK by MX Publishing
335 Princess Park Manor, Royal Drive,
London, N11 3GX
www.mxpublishing.com

Cover design by Brian Belanger

This book is dedicated to

Evelyn Herzog, ASH, BSI

friend of "the lads" and faithful reader of their chronicles

CONTENTS

Prologue
Another Fine Mess

"Murdered! Are you sure?"

"Pretty sure." *This ain't my first rodeo.* "Look at the blood on his right temple." I stood up and moved away so that Lynda could get a better view of the body.

My beloved being in no way squeamish, she looked. "Well, maybe he passed out and hit his head on the way down."

"Do you see anything around here that could cause a hole like that during a fall?"

She looked about briefly and then shook her lovely head. There wasn't much to see in the alcove. "No, I guess not. But killing him makes no sense at all."

"It must have made sense to somebody. Remember that question, 'Where do we hide the body?' I guess this is the answer, although it's a lousy one. This isn't very hidden, except for the fact that you and I are the only living people on the floor at the moment."

"So who are we supposed to call—hotel management or the police?"

Lynda wouldn't have asked that question if she hadn't been more discombobulated than she let on. Our duty as citizens to call 9-1-1 was clear. But I didn't respond. Instead, I said, "Well, I must say this is another fine mess Sebastian McCabe has gotten us into!"

"That's not fair, Jeff." She rolled her eyes. I wasn't looking at her to see this, but I know my Lynda. "Mac had nothing to do with you being here to begin with."

"No, but he could have found the body instead of me!"

Fairness compels me to admit, however, that she had spoken the truth. Mac was innocent, this time. For the person who had set off the chain of events ultimately responsible for my unfortunate presence on the scene of the crime was Lynda Teal (Cody) herself, my dear spouse and light of my life.

That had been months before . . .

Chapter One
Dead Writer Walking

Rex Carter, Lynda's favorite living mystery writer, was expected to soon lose that distinction. The living part, I mean. She informed me of this during cocktail hour in front of the fireplace at Chez Cody one cold winter day.

"He has lung cancer, and apparently in the last stages." She sipped her Manhattan. "I read about it on Facebook today. And the hot rumor is that he's killing off St. George to end the series on his way out."

I said a silent prayer of gratitude that Lynda had sworn off cigarettes some years before—silent because my frequent health warnings in her smoking days had not been well received. In fact, they had contributed to a regrettable hiatus in the Cody-Teal love story. So, instead of venturing into touchy territory, I said:

"Good riddance. About the end of the character, I mean."

Maybe you've read some of Carter's many Ian St. George thrillers. Even if you haven't, you probably know through general pop culture awareness that St. George is a British bloke who wears a black eyepatch and solves mysteries while elegantly freeloading his way through life— part Robin Hood and part vigilante. His anti-heroic charm had always eluded me. For one thing, eyepatches always remind me of Dr. Evil's assistant in *Austin Powers*. For another, I always thought the St. George setup was a bit gimmicky, especially his walking stick. Its inner workings changed from book to book, depending on what St. George needed it to be—gun, flask, leaded bludgeon, and so forth. Too clever by half, I say.

"Well, I like the character a lot," Lynda retorted, her husky voice pouty but cute. "And I like Carter's style. I'd love to see him at QueenCon before he passes. It's going to be so close to us this year, Jeff. Wouldn't it be fun to go?"

So, that was it!

The eleventh annual edition of QueenCon, the mystery convention named for Golden Age of Mystery icon Ellery Queen, was coming to Cincinnati in the spring. And the Queen City of the West, as Henry Wadsworth Longfellow had called it long ago, is only forty miles downriver from our little town of Erin. Sebastian McCabe, my brother-in-law and best friend, grew up there—to the limited extent that he ever grew up at all.

"Mac's mom could watch Donata for a couple of days."

Our darling daughter was just over a year old that winter and of an amiable disposition. She already favored her mother's looks, with the same curly hair of a honey-blond hue.

"So what do you think?" Lynda prodded, looking at me over the cocktail glass with the full force of her gold-flecked brown eyes.

I'd been married long enough not to point out that she'd asked a second question without giving me time to answer the first. So I considered the matter of attending QueenCon XI, but not for long. A relaxing weekend away from home could be just the thing Lynda needed right now. She'd been under a lot of work stress lately. Speculation ran rampant in the financial press that her employer, the Grier Media Group, would split its print and broadcast operations into separate companies. Gannett, Scripps, and other media giants had already done that, to plaudits from Wall Street. My darling's job as a sort of circuit rider for news quality at Grier Ohio NewsGroup took her into the newsrooms of both newspapers and TV stations, so an uncoupling of the two at Grier could make her an unemployment statistic. She didn't talk much about this sword of Damocles, but I knew that it was hanging over her.

"Yes, it would be fun to go," I said, "and I think we should do it. I've never been to QueenCon or Bouchercon, although I went to Magna cum Murder in Indiana years ago."

Lynda put down her Manhattan, joined me on the aptly named love seat, and expressed her gratitude in a non-verbal manner.

"Maybe this will inspire you to write mysteries again," she said after a few moments.

"Who knows?" But I doubted it. I hadn't thought much about my seven—or was it eight?—unpublished Max Cutter private eye novels in quite a while. Banging my ahead against a closed door had lost its appeal for me some time back. I had made peace with the fact that I would never be a successful fiction writer like Mac, whose soft-boiled Damon Devlin amateur sleuth mysteries sold as fast as he could write them. Between my day job as communications director of St. Benignus University and evenings and weekends chronicling the adventures of Sebastian McCabe, I keep busy enough.

"At any rate," I added, "I know that Mac and Kate are going as usual. In fact, Mac's on the host committee. We can carpool and save money on the gas." My sister (the "Kate" half of Mac and Kate) is an artist by training and profession. She isn't much of a mystery reader but she's her husband's greatest fan.

I picked up my tablet from the coffee table and accessed the QueenCon website to begin the registration process. It was a fairly glitzy site, with a sizeable picture of Rex Carter on the home page. But Carter wasn't the main focus of the conference hoopla.

"No way!"

"What?" Lynda leaned forward. I love it when she does that.

"Edward Seton. I thought he was dead, but look." I turned the tablet her way. "He's the guest of honor."

"He must be somebody special if he's the GOH. How come I never heard of him?"

"A lot of people haven't, I guess, but I loved the private eye novels he wrote in the 1950s and '60s. His shamus's name was Jason Darke."

"Sounds shady."

I was too busy waxing nostalgic to comment on my beloved's wordplay. "I must have read a dozen or more of the Darke books in college, one right after the other, when I should have been studying Russian history or Greek and Roman drama. They always wound up involving commies or Nazis plotting a comeback, stuff like that. I have the impression that Seton's work lost popularity around the time of the Vietnam War, even though he kept writing for a while. He must be about a hundred by now."

Not quite. My favorite search engine quickly turned up a bio that showed he was only ninety-two and had recently lost a leg to diabetes. "His work is now being made available to old and new readers in retro editions from Rue Morgue books, starting with *The Stainless Steel Trap* and *End Game*," I read aloud from Wikipedia. "More are scheduled."

"You sound excited."

"Let's just say there'll be something for both of us at this convention," I said as I completed the registration form and "Liked" the QueenCon page on Facebook.

In my enthusiasm for an old favorite writer, I didn't even notice what was on the agenda for the conference's opening night reception.

"Edward Seton doesn't get enough respect," I announced to my brother-in-law the next morning as I commandeered one of his chairs.

I'd already ordered the first two Jason Darke reprints.

Sebastian McCabe, a bearded mountain in a bow tie, looked up in surprise from the paperwork disaster that is his desk. I hadn't called ahead before strolling across campus to his office in Herbert Hall, so my presence was as unexpected as my literary pronouncement.

"Indeed he does not, old boy," Mac agreed. "Or, rather, it would be more accurate to say that he *has* not. There seems to be a flutter of critical and popular interest in the Seton *oeuvre* these days." As the Lorenzo Smythe Professor of Literature and one-person Popular Culture Department at St. Benignus, he would know about that. "And what brings about this perceptive observation of yours?"

"QueenCon—Lynda and I are going."

"Splendid!"

"Right. It was Lynda's idea. She has a thing for Rex Carter's drivel and he's apparently dying, but may hold on long enough for QueenCon. Anyway, I'm sure you're aware that Seton's the guest of honor."

Mac nodded his hirsute head. "Yes, this will be his first appearance at any mystery conference since a feminist walkout during his panel at Bouchercon sometime in the seventies."

"You see! Not enough respect."

"Doubtless he feels like a pariah, Jefferson. The mystery community has not warmly embraced him because of his inelegant prose, sadistic story lines, and extreme political views, as well as the perceived sexism." *Is that all?* "His good friend, the late Mickey Spillane, suffered a similar literary exile for far too long."

"In other words," I cut to the chase, "he isn't personally popular among the mystery literati."

Mac chuckled, giving his chins a workout. "I have always admired your gift for understatement. I am fairly sure it would not be an exaggeration to say that some of those who will be in attendance at QueenCon loathe Edward Seton. I am not among them, having had some friendly correspondence with him over the years and a convivial meeting once when I happened to visit the town where he lives in Pennsylvania."

I stood up. "Well, at least nobody's going to kill him. I mean, nobody would do that at a conference of mystery writers and readers, right? That would be just too hokey."

Chapter Two
Whispers

". . . and to pursue the mysteries of life with you, hand in hand as your soulmate and partner, as long as our love shall last," the bride repeated.

"Then it is my great joy," the officiant declared, "to solemnize this union and pronounce you spouse and spouse."

The large room set aside for private parties just off the rotunda of the Cincinnati Union Terminal exploded with the enthusiastic applause of people eager to get on to the open-bar reception.

It was the opening night of QueenCon XI. You may be wondering how matrimony and mystery fiction fit together. So did I, when I finally got around to studying the convention schedule in greater depth a couple of weeks before the event. But Lynda, whose reading tastes in the crime genre are more wide-ranging than mine, had recognized the names of both the bride and the groom.

"Marcus Garber writes a delicious cozy series about a New Orleans chef and amateur sleuth, Pierre LeGrande," she'd informed me as she changed a diaper. "And Lisa Ballantine does those Kim Braxton police procedurals that I've been trying to get you to read. Apparently they got engaged at QueenCon X."

"How romantic."

"I guess so. But I still think it's kind of tacky, getting married in an old train station."

"That's because you're an old-fashioned church wedding kind of gal, Lyn. It's more than just an old train station, though. The Terminal is iconic."

"At least it won't be as tawdry as that *Star Wars*-themed wedding in Hollywood when *The Force Awakens* premiered a few months back."

And it wasn't. The officiant on that final Friday in April was actually a clergyman in his day job—a Humanistic rabbi named Brian Adelmann from upstate in Canton, Ohio. Appropriately, he writes mysteries on the side. His Israeli private detective is constantly getting on the wrong side of the law for political reasons, exposing some of the internal tensions in the Jewish State. I'd read all three novels in the series so far, finding them surprisingly entertaining. The rabbi himself was also a surprise. With a slight build and wispy beard, he didn't look old enough to have entered a rabbinical seminary, much less graduated. I bet he got carded a lot.

Marcus Garber, making more than a nod to tradition, wore tails but no top hat. He was a huge guy in his late thirties with a shaved head and a round gold earring on his left ear. I thought he looked more like a WWE wrestler or a prison guard than a mystery writer—especially one who wrote about a chef. His just-pronounced wife, somewhat younger, was a petite blonde, very short but with long hair cascading over a strapless Victorian wedding gown.

"What a beautiful dress," Lynda commented as the newlyweds kissed to continued applause.

"Not as beautiful as yours on a similar occasion." And I would have said that even if Lynda hadn't sewed her own gown for our nuptials five years earlier.[1] I squeezed my bride's hand as a cellist played "Ode to Joy" and the couple walked down a carpet of rose petals strewn in the aisle between the rows of folding chairs.

---

[1] See *The 1895 Murder*, MX Publishing, 2012.

With the service concluded, everybody fanned out into the terminal rotunda for the reception, sponsored by the League of Indie Crime Writers. (What a deal! I wish somebody else had sponsored our wedding party.) A couple of hundred mystery writers and their fans sipped drinks and munched on cookies and wedding cake under the largest half-dome in the western hemisphere. To be fair, the wedding couple had supplied the cake.

Most of the men present had dressed up in suits or sport coats and the women largely in cocktail dresses, which in some cases showed off tattoos not normally seen. But body art doesn't interest me. I found myself gawking instead at the venue, built in the early 1930s to handle more than 200 trains and thousands of passengers every day. Now Union Terminal houses the several museums of the Cincinnati Museum Center. I'd only been in the art deco wonder a few times, mostly for exhibits of mummies and whatnot that Kate and Lynda wanted to see. And once I came for the model train display.

The building itself is a kind of museum, decorated with huge mosaic murals on the north and south sides of the rotunda portraying American progress, advances in transportation from rafts to airplanes, and the march of Cincinnati history. Still, it had been built as a train station. How many soldiers, sailors, and marines had boarded trains here in the 1940s on their way to war and back? And how many never came back?

"You're still wishing you hadn't given away your toy train set, aren't you?" Kate said, breaking into my thoughts.

"They're *model* trains, not toys," I corrected. Why can my sister never get that right?

I'd passed my trains on to Amanda, Kate and Mac's younger daughter, years before. Now fifteen, my precocious niece had just started working on college applications and her second opera. *Maybe she's no longer interested in my—Wait a minute!*

"It isn't just a set," I told Kate sternly. "It's a whole town, with trees and everything. It's awesome." That is not a word I use lightly.

Almost as tall as my six-one and with the same shade of red hair but much longer, Kate regarded Lynda with feigned exasperation. At least, I think it was feigned. "You can keep him."

My wife, her hair fetchingly done up in a French braid and her shapely form draped in a clingy dress of bright spring colors, grabbed my free hand. "That's good, because I'm not giving him up."

Can we go to our hotel room now?

Before my sister could spoil the magic of the moment, Mac beat her to it by reminding all of us that the Union Terminal building had been the model for the Hall of Justice on the *Super Friends* TV show and later incorporated into the DC Comics universe. I knew that. I also knew that there's one big difference between the cartoon/comics version of the building and the real thing: The façade of the Hall of Justice, unlike the Terminal, doesn't have a huge clock.

As Mac droned on, I tuned out and looked around at the milling and munching crowd of mystery mavens. They came in all shapes, sizes, and modes of dress. One couple, male and female, wore matching deerstalker caps. Several women wore outlandish chapeaux of all different sorts, including a black leather fedora, and one gent hid his hair (if any) under a cowboy hat. A woman in a sweater dress had wrapped a yellow and black scarf in a "crime scene" tape design around her neck. She was peering over her plastic glass at a lean specimen sporting a pencil-thin mustache and a black eyepatch. If he was trying to look like Rex Carter's Ian St. George, I thought, he should have carried a walking stick. But maybe he just had a bad eye.

"Do you see any celebrities?" Lynda asked. Mac had wound down, so she no longer had to listen politely.

"Does Alexian Rowe count?"

Rowe, tall and lean with long black hair combed straight back and a neat goatee, owns Crimes & Punishments Bookshop in New York. I'd met him the previous year at the shop.[2] He apparently hadn't changed the purple orchid in the lapel of his three-piece suit since then. He was raising a glass to a stout fellow who reminded me of Alfred Hitchcock, except alive.

"No," Lynda replied. "At least, he's not a celebrity in my universe."

"Then not yet. I can't even tell the writers from the readers unless their nametags are facing my way."

Said nametags were color-coded—blood red for the writers, green for the fans. Speakers and panelists also had a yellow ribbon attached to the tag.

"Look at the eyepatch."

I started to say that I already had, but then I realized that Lynda was nodding toward a woman who appeared to be listening intently to a man maybe forty years her senior, with a thick gray mustache and no hair on his dome. The woman wore long, platinum blond hair, parted in the middle, and a short gray dress above red high heels. The eyepatch on her right eye was white. With the heels, she was almost as tall as my six-one.

"She must be the anti-St. George," I joked, "with a white eyepatch instead of black. Maybe she—"

"It's him!" Lynda interrupted ungrammatically, grabbing my arm.

Somehow I sensed that this moment of excitement was the wrong time to correct her English.

"Him as in who?" *Or should that be "whom"? I always have trouble with that one.*

"Rex Carter! That man she's talking to is Rex Carter himself."

---

[2] See *Bookmarked for Murder*, MX Publishing, 2015.

Be still my beating heart.

"He does not look well," Mac observed. "Note the grayness of his skin and the wrinkles. The ravages of cancer and chemotherapy are sadly obvious. The last time I saw Rex he looked like a completely different person."

"At least the hair of his mustache didn't fall out," I said in a doomed attempt at one-upmanship.

"The mustache is false."

"Then why doesn't he wear a wig? He doesn't have any hair on his head, either."

"He never did," Lynda said. "At least, not in his picture on the books I've read."

"You should introduce yourself to him," I suggested. *He may die before breakfast.*

"He's busy, Jeff. That woman is obviously a big fan."

"So are you. I'll hold your Manhattan."

"I could take it with me. And I guess I will."

So she sashayed over to join the party. I watched her retreating derriere with husbandly interest.

"Did you see Ned Seton?" Mac asked.

I snapped around. "No! Where?"

"Near the bar on the left, being attended by Lafcadio Figg."

Spotting Figg was easy. The retired high school drama teacher affects muttonchops among his other eccentricities. A former Cincinnatian now resident in Erin, he served with Mac on the host committee for QueenCon. Despite their shared interest in Sherlock Holmes and membership in some of the same Holmes societies, or perhaps because of it, those two mix like oil and beer. Whether Figg moved to Erin just to bedevil Mac is anybody's guess, and I could bet either way. They are brothers under the skin, though, and their rivalry is of the sibling sort.

Figg stood next to a wheelchair. In the chair sat, or rather leaned, an old man with white hair cut in a military crewcut. With some imagination I could recognize him as a much older version of the Edward Seton whose photo I'd found in my Internet research the previous winter.

"And you said *Carter* didn't look well," I murmured to Mac.

Without waiting for a rejoinder, I walked over to the aged writer. There's only one way to do the old meet-and-greet with authors, so I embraced it.

"Mr. Seton? I've enjoyed your books for years."

"Well, I've been around for years." His voice was suitably gravelly, although spirited. "In fact, most of my fans are quite a bit older than you, I'm afraid."

"I began reading you in the nineties, before you were popular again." *Extra points for that!* I saw no point in mentioning that I'd stopped reading him after a binge that took me through the first couple of decades of his work. I'd never gotten around to reading them again even though I'd bought the two reprints on that winter day. And maybe that's just as well: Early loves encountered in later life sometimes disappoint.

"You are a very discerning reader, Jeff, if you are a fan of Jason Darke," said Lafcadio Figg. He didn't mean it, though. He just wanted to say something. I doubted that he'd ever actually read any of Seton's Darke yarns, which were probably a bit gritty for the former teacher's refined tastes.

"Hello, Sebastian," he added.

"Hello, Lafcadio." The two rivals were seldom anything other than coldly polite to each other. Mac addressed himself to the man in the wheelchair. "Hello, Edward. I am glad that you could be here."

"Hell, I'm glad that I can be anywhere."

Seton had curmudgeon down pat, but then he'd probably been working on it for years. Mac introduced me to him as his friend, brother-in-law, and Boswell (which I hate, but not as much as I hate being called his Watson). I pulled my copy of *The Stainless Steel Trap* out of my sport coat pocket. "Would you please autograph this for me?"

He squinted at the provocatively posed and scantily clad brunette on the front of the paperback, facing down a Colt .45 in the beefy hand of handsome-ugly Jason Darke. Darke wore a fedora. "I've always loved that cover. But you didn't pick this up in the nineties. It's the new reprint."

My mother, the poet Cornelia Randolph Cody, had found and confiscated my used paperback copy of that classic on one of my visits home during college. (Fortunately, I'd already read it.) But I didn't think Seton would want to hear that, so I just said, "More royalties for you! I'm glad to see you back in print. I also have *End Game.*"

He smiled and scrawled, *"Re-read it and weep, Jeff. Your favorite writer, Ned Seton."*

What a card.

As he handed the book back to me, Seton's eyes brightened and he straightened up as he looked over my shoulder. I turned around to see what had attracted his attention. Or rather, who. I didn't blame him for perking up at the sight of her. That happens to me every day, but not because of some shallow physical interest. Well, not entirely.

"Have a drink." Lynda handed me a beer. I had acquired something of a taste for Manhattans from drinking them for Linda while she'd been pregnant, but if I drink more than one or two I can't be responsible for what comes out of my mouth. Beer is safer for me at public events, and not a lot of it. I had a twelve-pack of Caffeine-Free Diet Coke back in our hotel room. Nobody can convince me that caffeine is healthy, no matter what those studies say.

"This is my wife, Lynda Teal Cody," I told Seton. *Hands off. Eyes off, too. Advanced age is no excuse.*

He responded with the usual niceties. Just then the crowd began moving back to the scene of the nuptials, like a herd of buffalo. During the reception, the flower petals from the wedding had been swept off the floor and a large screen lowered from the ceiling. It was movie time for our happy confab.

"How was Carter?" I asked Lynda as we walked back to the private room, hand in hand, for the screening.

"After about ten minutes of listening to him get his arm talked off by that platinum blonde fangirl—I'm almost sure it's a wig, by the way—I gave up. She kept insisting that the main female character in the St. George novel *Cat's-paw* must have been based on a real person and he kept denying it. Immovable object meeting irresistible force."

"Occupational hazard of the successful fictioneer, I guess. I should be so lucky. Well, he'll be around all weekend." *If the Big C doesn't take him out in mid-conference.*

Apparently in homage to the other main event of the evening, the convention committee chose *The Bride Wore Black* as the Friday night flick. That's a 1968 François Truffaut film (serious directors like him make films, not movies) about a woman who sets out to kill five men she doesn't know. Why? That's the mystery.

"Well, that was a real upper," Lynda said afterward. Sometimes I confuse irony and sarcasm, but I'm pretty sure that was both. And so was: "I bet the bride and groom loved it. That should put them in a great mood for the wedding night."

"I guess that depends on whether they're into *film noir*," I said.

"Oh, yes, *film noir*—that's French for 'we're screwed,' isn't it?"

See why I love that woman?

"That about sums it up," I agreed. Mac would have taken a lot more words to say the same thing. My brother-in-law had skipped *The Bride Wore Black* in favor of a party in the hospitality-room suite of his publisher, Dog in the Night-Time Press. "Let's walk around a little before we go back to the hotel."

An architecture critic had once written in *The New York Times* that Union Terminal made Radio City Music Hall look like a toy. I don't know about that, but the vastness and the grandeur of the thing made me feel like a kid. And kids love nothing more than ice cream. I peered in the door of the closed Rookwood Ice Cream Parlor, with the name spelled out in green and red neon lights. The floor and walls were all made of Rookwood tile, a Cincinnati brand name so well known to pottery collectors that it's almost a generic term for decorative tile. Or so Kate tells me, and she would know. A sign informed us that the parlor served Graeter's, and the Cincinnati-based Graeter's brand is to ice cream as Rookwood is to pottery.

"It's too bad—"

I stopped because I heard a female voice, speaking in a near-whisper.

"Where do we hide the body?"

An answer, if that's what it was, came in the form of a *"sssssh"* sound, followed by a giggle.

I looked around.

The speaker was nowhere to be seen. Lynda and I were alone at that end of the concourse.

Chapter Three
Bad Blood

"Did you hear that?"

"I did if you did," Lynda said, "because that means I'm not crazy. Do you think it was the ghost of somebody who died here when it was a train station?"

"Not unless ghosts giggle, and somehow I doubt that. But I know what we heard and I know what we didn't see, namely whoever was talking."

"So it's a mystery. Mac will love it."

But we didn't see Mac until we were almost finished with breakfast Saturday morning in the Garfield Room of the Fountain Square Hotel, ready for QueenCon XI to get underway in earnest. By that time, we had ruled out an invisible woman of both the H.G. Wells variety and the G.K. Chesterton type, the latter being someone that we simply didn't notice (such as a server or bartender).

"I still think it could have been an aspiring ventriloquist throwing her voice," Lynda insisted as she slathered artery-clogging butter on her toast. That was a trope from a different Chesterton story, by the way. And I had been less than enthused when she'd first tried this idea on me about three o'clock that morning. How could she look so awake just five hours later, smiling and decked out in a gold and chocolate dress that matched her eyes?

"Possibly," I said with a yawn, going back to my Greek yogurt. April showers beat against the restaurant window, through which we had a third-floor view of

Fountain Square in the heart of the Queen City's compact downtown.

"In which case, we wouldn't have to worry about stumbling across a hidden body somewhere," my beloved added triumphantly.

"I'll drink to that." I popped the tab on the can of Caffeine-Free Diet Coke that I'd brought from our room. I don't know why so few restaurants have it on tap. "I'm sure you have the right idea. Nothing else makes sense."

With that, I gave myself over to people-watching our fellow conventioneers and inventing stories about them.

"See the tall woman with the almost-orange hair, kind of built like a stork?" I said sotto voce. "I bet she's an extreme couponer. She probably killed her husband in an argument over who got the use of their last kid's bedroom after he moved off to college. She wanted it for the coupons and he saw it as a man cave."

Lynda nodded thoughtfully, chewing her ham-and-bacon-stuffed omelet doused with hot sauce. "And now she doesn't know where to hide the body. You could be right, darling. But, on the other hand, she could be one of the toxicologists on that poison panel. She looks like the picture of Dr. Jane Redken in the program."

And so on. The early arrivals to the restaurant finished their breakfast and moved on, replaced by those—like my sister and her husband—who had slept in. Our fellow mystery mavens ran the gamut from the aging baby boomer guy in the vintage "Sgt. Pepper's Lonely Hearts Club Band" T-shirt, to the slender young woman wearing a cloche hat, to the pony-tailed man about my age dressed in a pinstriped gray suit and a tie.

"The newlyweds are here," I commented as they walked in, both wearing jeans.

"They look sleepy," Lynda snickered. Before I could craft a witty retort worthy of a man suffering sleep deprivation for non-romantic reasons, my smartphone rang.

"Talk to me," I said in my best Kojak voice, which isn't very good. This mystery weekend deal was getting to me already. Lynda rolled her eyes.

"It's Decker."

"Oh, no."

Lt. Ed Decker, of Campus Security at St. Benignus University, never called me with good news.

"Daley said I should call you."

Cal Daley, a former assistant police chief in Cincinnati, had been chief of security at the Forty Thieves Casino in Cincinnati[3] before being hired for the newly created position of Director of Public Safety at St. Benignus. Someday I may tell you why we needed one, but I'm not over the PTSD yet. Let's just say it involved a large financial settlement by the university.

"Nice of Cal to think of me."

"Yeah. He says hi." I imagined the look of impatience on Decker's broad, black face. "Do you remember a girl named Lani Alvarez?"

"How could I ever forget?"

Ms. Alvarez was the leader, if that was the word, of the Young Socialist Brigade at St. Benignus. (Can anarchists have a leader?) The neo-Trotskyite group had been decertified as a campus organization because of its avowedly atheist constitution, but that wasn't even a speed bump for Alvarez. Official fiats were high on the list of things she had no use for, right up there with bras.

"Right," Decker said. "She's memorable. Well, one of my officers arrested her this morning during a protest against student fees going to athletics."

Only the timing surprised me. The allegedly high student fees and how much of that went to sports teams had been a hot issue on campus the month before because of a series of stories in *The Spectator*, our student newspaper.

---

[3] See "Dogs Don't Make Mistakes" in *Rogues Gallery*, MX Publishing, 2014.

But Alvarez had been wrapped up in another cause at the time.[4]

"Where's the headline in that, Ed? Alvarez only gets arrested on days ending in 'y.'"

"This time she's claiming police brutality."

Oh. Why hadn't she ever thought of that before?

I repressed a sigh. "What happened?" Job one for me in dealing with a controversial situation at the university is to get the facts straight. If I make a public statement that's not true in every detail, however innocent the inaccuracy on my part, somebody will nail me on it and give the story new legs. That's guaranteed.

"Officer Jackson says she got in his face very aggressively. He felt threatened, so he shoved her back. She says he 'personhandled' her. I swear, that's what she called it—'personhandled.' She's plastering Facebook and Twitter with a picture of a bruise on her arm. Of course, that doesn't prove Jackson had anything to do with it."

"What does the video from the security cameras show?"

"It's ambiguous where it counts, just like a lot of surveillance video. Alvarez is screaming at Jackson for sure, but it's going to take some expert doing a frame-by-frame analysis to see exactly what he did, if anything, that caused her to blow up."

"Is he on desk duty?"

I could imagine Decker nodding. "Administrative leave, we call it."

"Outside investigation underway?"

"Will be. Daley's calling Hummel."

Oscar Hummel, Erin's police chief and a good buddy to Mac and me, would immediately assign his assistant chief, Lt. Col. L. Jack Gibbons, to the task. And

---

[4] See *Erin Go Bloody*, MX Publishing, 2016.

Gibbons never screws up. Never. If Officer Jackson hadn't gone over the line, he had nothing to worry about.

The talking points were already forming in my head in anticipation of my first media call: "St. Benignus University takes this accusation, like all allegations of impropriety by employees, quite seriously. Officer Jackson has been placed . . ."

Lynda leaned across the breakfast table, her gold earrings dangling, and pantomimed an exaggerated kiss. I forgot the rest of the second talking point.

"Uh, Jeff?" Decker said. If I didn't know him, I would have said he sounded embarrassed. "There's one more thing you probably ought to know. Jackson and Alvarez had a relationship."

"You mean he'd arrested her before?"

"I think he did, but that's not what I meant. They used to date."

"Date!" *Do they still call it that?* "Are you sure, Ed? I don't think Alvarez likes men, and I know damned well she doesn't like cops."

"Right on both counts. Apparently that caused a little tension in their relationship. Jackson didn't like being told at the send-off that he'd been a sociological experiment."

You can't make this stuff up.

"Lovely. Well, if you get any media calls, just send them my way."

"With pleasure. Have a nice weekend, Jeff."

How can I not? "You too."

I disconnected.

"What was that all about?" Lynda asked.

"Just a minor kerfuffle back at the ranch. No big crisis. Turn off your journalist genes and relax." *As if you could.* I looked around the restaurant. "Color-coding the authors' nametags is a good idea, but they could refine it by the type of mystery. Take the lady in the tangerine sweater. I bet she writes cozies, which is just a cute name for romance novels with a couple of murders tossed in. Maybe her nametag should be pink or lavender." Lynda looked a couple of tables over, where the woman was sitting by herself. She wore round glasses exactly the same color as the bulky turtleneck. I thought she looked a little like Velma on *Scooby-Doo*, but with darker and shorter hair. She carried a canvas handbag roughly the size of my rarely driven Volkswagen New Beetle.

"Cozies always have something to do with a coffee house or crocheting," I pontificated, "and the female amateur sleuth always has a boyfriend who's a cop."

"He isn't *always* a cop, darling."

"In all those books you made me read, he was."

She smiled at me over her mug of caffeine-laced coffee. "I could never make Jeff Cody do anything." *Liar.* "I just thought you'd enjoy them. They're light entertainment."

"Lighter than air, but I didn't find them entertaining. You know my taste runs more to the hard-boiled side of the house."

"You're about as hard-boiled as a chocolate Easter egg with French cream filling."

Is that a good thing or a bad thing?

"One cannot argue taste, old boy," a familiar voice boomed behind me. "Or at least, one should not."

Mac and Kate slid into the seats we'd reserved for them. Himself, who knows the meaning of every word in the dictionary except "informal," wore a bow tie about the same bright shade of yellow as Lynda's Mustang, splattered with navy blue polka dots. Kate had donned the Sherlock Holmes necktie from our London adventure a few years earlier, never mind that she planned to spend most of the day (and a lot of money) shopping in downtown Cincinnati. I hoped that Saks and Tiffany's, both less than a block away, were braced for the assault.

"Good afternoon," I told Mac, by way of exaggerating his late arrival. "We've got a mystery for you."

"It kept me up most the night," Lynda said brightly.

(Insert your own sarcastic and/or salacious Codyism here.)

"How intriguing! Please expound."

I told the tale as dramatically as I could muster, letting my voice sink into a whisper as I quoted, "*Where do we hide the body?*"

"And when we looked around"—I paused—"*there was nobody there!*"

Mac chuckled.

"This is no joke," I said crossly, "and I'm not making it up."

"I am sure that you are not, Jefferson. I am equally sure that you were standing near a water fountain."

I thought back. In my mind's eye I could see a tile fountain, maybe Rookwood, in a corner to the left of the ice cream parlor.

"Oooh, something's coming back to me," Lynda said, "something about the acoustics of that place."

"Precisely!" Mac said. "Stand near the drinking fountain at one end of the Union Terminal rotunda and whisper sweet nothings which can be heard quite clearly by your lover far away on the other end. Couples and friends have been doing that for nearly three-quarters of a century. The sound bounces off the arch and continues bouncing off the curved surface all the way to the top of the arch, one hundred and six feet up, and down to the other person at the matching drinking fountain on the other side."

Maybe it would be unfair to call the McCabe expression smug, but he certainly seemed quite pleased with himself at imparting this bit of Queen City trivia.

"How do you know that?" I demanded.

Sebastian McCabe may be a genius in matters literary and criminal—if you don't believe me, just ask him—but science has never been his strong suit.

"Very simple, old boy. An explanation of 'The Whisper Gallery' is posted above each fountain."

"Humph. Well, we were talking last night, not reading. And anyway, more importantly, what we heard wasn't exactly a lover murmuring sweet nothings."

"Is it so surprising that two mystery writers would engage in a spot of book plotting during the QueenCon reception?"

"Then you don't think—" Lynda began.

"Good morning, fellow Erinites!"

"Good morning, Lafcadio," Mac told his mutton-chopped antagonist. *Is it cold in here, or is it just you?* "I really must congratulate you once again on having the vision to bring QueenCon to Cincinnati." Mac talked as if every word of praise hurt him to utter.

Figg, whose coat sleeves were too long for his stubby body, bowed theatrically, as befit his former career in drama. "I had an excellent committee. Thank you for your work on that."

This was painful to watch and to hear. Any minute they would break into a chorus of "Kumbaya." They needed an intervention, so I provided it.

"How in the world did you get Ned Seton to come?" I asked Figg.

"It wasn't easy, Jeff. We worked through Paul Malvern."

I knew that name from some reading I'd done in anticipation of QueenCon. Malvern, an academic type, had recently been designated as Rex Carter's official biographer. But he'd also done much to create interest in Seton within the groves of academe, almost single-handedly making the creator of Jason Darke fair game for serious treatment as "an American original."

"The really hard part was getting Seton to let Rex Carter introduce him as the guest of honor this afternoon. There's some sort of bad blood between them. I suspect a woman was involved."

"Only one?" I quipped. Carter had a reputation as a womanizer.

Lynda rolled her eyes.

"Maybe I should come back for that when I've cleaned out Saks," Kate said, putting her handbag on her shoulder. "I love fireworks."

Chapter Four
Hard Boiled

After Kate had departed on her shopping spree, Mac joined me at the panel on "Private Eyes and Other Hard-Boiled Guys" in Parlor G on the fourth floor. Lynda deserted me for one of the other two panels, "The Logical Successor: Ellery Queen and Sherlock Holmes." Mac would have chosen that as well, but Ned Seton was listed in the program as one of the hard-boiled panelists and Mac wanted to hear him.

"I'm surprised Velma's at this one," I murmured to Mac as we settled ourselves in our chairs.

"Eh?"

I nodded toward the front of the room. "See the woman in the tangerine sweater and the huge canvas handbag—the one talking to the guy with the three-day beard? I call her Velma because she reminds me of that character on *Scooby-Doo*, the brainy one. Ten bucks says she writes a cozy series about the owner of a teashop or some such. I bet she wandered into the wrong panel."

Fortunately for me, Sebastian McCabe eschews gambling. Within about a minute, both the woman in question and her conversation partner, who had long brown hair and a sharp nose, moved to the head of the room. They sat down in the two remaining chairs at a long table, meaning they weren't lost after all. The only panelist I recognized was Seton, whose wheelchair was wedged in at one end of the table.

The guy who was saving on razor blades slid over a microphone so that it was in front of him. "Good morning. If you're looking for 'Private Eyes and Other Hard-Boiled Guys,' you have the right room. My name is Paul Malvern. I teach at Bowling Green State University here in Ohio and I've written extensively about mystery fiction. My current project is a biography of Rex Carter. I'm really excited by the panel we have for you this morning. It's a special privilege to have with us the guest of honor here at QueenCon XI, Ned Seton. As I'm sure most of you know, Mr. Seton is the creator of Cold War detective Jason Darke. This weekend marks his first appearance at a mystery con in his long career."

After a round of applause for that, eliciting a grudging nod from Seton in his wheelchair, Malvern introduced the other panelists and asked them to say a little about their books: Julio Diaz, creator of Miami bounty-hunter Danny Ortega; Grant Pogue, who writes about disbarred attorney-turned-PI Eddie Quick; and Melanie Swann, who described herself as "author of the Birdy Edwards historical mysteries and several unpublished plays."

Mac raised an eyebrow at that last named, who was the woman in the turtleneck sweater. His gesture could have meant anything—or nothing.

I made the mental adjustment from "Velma" to "Melanie," but it was still hard to picture her writing about "a two-fisted Pinkerton detective in the rough-and-tumble world of the late nineteenth century." That's how the Birdy Edwards series was described in the program, which I had thumbed through again as Malvern talked. The series amounted to five books so far, the latest of which called *The End of the Line*. I hadn't heard of them, but there are a lot of mysteries out there. I had read and liked a few of the Danny Ortega books, though, and I'd just finished Pogue's *Quick and the Undead*, a satire on the zombie craze.

"The first question I'd like to ask each of you is 'why PI?'" Malvern said. "Why not write about a cop or an amateur detective?"

"Cops!" Seton rasped, speaking out of turn. "Who needs 'em? They have to play by the rules, and the rules favor the criminals. By the time a cop reads the bad guy his rights, the bastard's killed somebody else. I never messed with cops in my books, except as a foil for Darke. He never read anybody their rights."

"Asshole," muttered a guy on my left with close-cropped hair, probably a cop.

Seton's quip got a few nervous laughs from others in the audience, but not many. Maybe it hit a little too close to home, what with several controversial cases of "police-involved shootings" (cliché of the day) in the news of late. Julio Diaz sat back a bit, I noticed.

"A private eye seems like a more realistic choice as a detective hero than an amateur for the purposes of fiction, even though he's actually not," opined Grant Pogue. "But at the same time, he has more freedom than a sworn officer of the law." Pogue was a grandfatherly type in a suit and tie, wearing a gray mustache he had swiped off a walrus. "I'm a judge in my day job, but I get a kick out of having Eddie Quick do all kinds of things that I would have thrown the book at him for when I was a prosecutor."

His fellow panelists smiled at the admission, even Seton. They'd probably all been there themselves, in one way or another.

"Danny Ortega isn't a private eye, but he might as well be," said Diaz, a dark-complexioned man who appeared to be a little younger than me, say late thirties. He had a great voice for radio, rich and precise. "I was inspired by Raymond Chandler—not so much by his fiction as by his essay, 'The Simple Art of Murder.' That's the one where he says, 'down these mean streets a man must go who is not himself mean, who is neither tarnished nor afraid. He is the hero; he is everything. He must be a complete man and a common man and yet an unusual man.' Then at the end he says, 'If there were enough like him, the world would be a very safe place to live in, without becoming too dull to be worth living in.' That's the kind of man Danny Ortega is, a knight in rusty armor. The biggest difference between him and similar characters is that he came to the United States from Cuba in a leaky boat when he was three years old. By a strange coincidence, so did I."

Note to self: Dust off Chandler and re-read.

Melanie Swann moved the microphone in front of her. "My books are private eye novels by definition because they are about a private detective. Sherlock Holmes and Nero Wolfe are also private detectives, but in many ways they act just like amateur sleuths who are completely free agents. They are very independent." ("A fair point," Mac rumbled to himself.) "Nothing wrong with that, of course. It's who they are. But I thought it would be fun to have a detective who's more of a working man. Birdy Edwards is a Pinkerton agent. He reports to a boss, not just to the client. And he's a manly man, kind of the father I never had."

Calling Dr. Freud!

"But you didn't invent the character. He came from Conan Doyle's *The Valley of Fear*," Malvern prodded.

"That's right. It's the last Sherlock Holmes novel and my favorite, even though it's highly underrated by most readers. The second half of the book is a hard-boiled detective story, maybe the world's first."

Holmes again! Is there no escaping that man? If Lynda were here, she'd be trying not to smirk and failing miserably. Mac didn't even try not to. I studiously ignored the look on his bearded face.

"But that's not where I started with the first book in my series, *The Fat of the Land*," Swann said. "My original concept was to write about an American private investigator working in the nineteenth century when law enforcement didn't have the advantages of the crime lab or the disadvantages of Miranda warnings." Her eyes slid briefly in Seton's direction. "And then I thought, 'Why reinvent the eye?' Conan Doyle already gave us the perfect hero for that time and milieu in the person of Birdy Edwards, who worked for the original private eye—Allan Pinkerton."

Malvern looked fascinated. Or, he looked like somebody who was trying to look fascinated. I couldn't tell. "My next question was going to be what writer influenced you most, but I guess you've already answered that."

"You're thinking Conan Doyle?" Melanie Swann shook her head. "Actually, I'd have to say my father was the writer who influenced me most."

"Your father was a writer?"

"Oh, yes. He wrote my mother a note to tell her it was nice meeting her. She never saw him again, but she kept that note until the day she died."

The room went still. Malvern blinked a few times, caught seriously off guard, until Julio Diaz rescued him by picking up on the question.

"Influence is a funny thing," he said. "Chandler inspired me, like I said, but Walter Mosley influenced me more because he was a black man writing about a black man, Easy Rawlins. If he could do that, why couldn't a Cuban-American write about a Cuban-American? Plus, he sold a lot of books and I wanted to sell a lot of books. I still do."

"Don't count on it, sonny," Seton said. "No offense." If you really want to offend somebody, be sure to say "no offense." For extra credit, call a grown man "sonny." The look on Diaz's face was murderous. I could see why Seton wasn't the most popular member of the Mystery Writers of America (if he was a member, which I doubted), and it had nothing to do with his subtle-as-a-sledgehammer writing style. "The real money is in breaking out of the pack like the Mick"—Mickey Spillane, I assumed—"did back in the forties. He sold millions of Mike Hammer books in hardback. That's what caused me to start pecking away at the old Underwood on my first Jason Darke. But who can break out today?"

Well, let's see. There's Harlan Coben, David Baldacci, Stuart Woods, Janet Evanovich, John Grisham, Lee Child, James Patterson, Patricia Cornwell, Douglas Preston & Lincoln Child . . . Their books are shelved with mysteries at most libraries. You'll also find them on the *New York Times* best-seller list.

My mind started to drift. "*Where do we hide the body?*" Mac's idea that Lynda and I had overheard two plotting mystery writers made perfect sense. I mean, talk about hiding bodies could be normal conversation for a mystery con, right? But still . . . It was a woman's voice. I eyed Melanie Swann suspiciously. She didn't look like a killer. She looked like Velma. Clearly, this was getting out of hand. Sometimes my mind has a mind of its own.

When I tuned into the panel again, Judge Pogue had the floor.

"Gardner's Perry Mason novels are practically forgotten now. They're not in print and there's nothing like a Baker Street Irregulars or a Wolfe Pack for Mason. But they were incredibly popular in their day, and so was the TV show with Raymond Burr. That show is what inspired me to be a lawyer. Later, I read the books. Mason was as hardboiled as any private eye, especially in the earlier novels. And the Bertha Cool–Donald Lam books that Gardner wrote under the pseudonym of A.A. Fair . . ."

And so forth.

The Q&A session elicited the usual Q's and the usual A's: "What's more important to you: plot or character?" "Do you outline?" "How long were you writing before you made your first sale?"

A buxom woman in a purple hat, her age somewhere north of sixty, wanted to know why Melanie

Swann didn't write about a female protagonist. "A number of women have done that," the inquisitor pointed out.

"And a number of women haven't," Swann politely fired back. "Gender wasn't an issue for me, or at least not the gender of my protagonist. I imagine Christie felt the same way, and she did okay. There were female private detectives in the nineteenth century, so I could have gone down that road. But women didn't beat people up in those days and I felt that was too much of a limitation for my protagonist."

I made a mental note to give one of her books a road test soon.

Mac stood up, just in case anybody failed to see his Falstaffian figure or hear his stentorian voice. "What is the best advice each of you ever received as a writer?"

Seton didn't hesitate and he didn't need a microphone. "Keep writing. Ignore the naysayers, ignore your wife and/or girlfriend, ignore the editors who turn you down—ignore anybody who tells you you're no good. You probably aren't, but keep at it until you are."

While the other panelists delivered the same message in different packaging, I thought about that. Maybe I'd given up too soon on my Max Cutter novels. All of those panelists had gotten published. In fact, QueenCon was full of people who'd gotten published! If they could do it, why couldn't I? Things had changed a lot since I'd last sent out a manuscript. One of the changes was the rise of the independent writer, as in the League of Indie Crime Writers. I could be my own publisher! The idea had a certain appeal. Why should a publisher get ninety percent of my book's sales price when I wrote it?

"One last question!" Malvern announced.

The guy next to me, with the short hair and no sideburns, raised his hand. He didn't look happy. He hadn't looked happy for about twenty minutes. "I'm a police officer, Mr. Seton, and I didn't appreciate—"

No surprise there, I thought, just as my smartphone pinged. I looked down at a text message from Decker. *Media wolves are circling. Expect calls.*

Job security, I texted back.

Rewriting my old Max Cutter books might be tough in view of the march of technology in the last few years, I mused. Maybe I should start from scratch. How about the murder of a campus protestor disguised to look like police brutality?

Chapter Five
What Golden Age?

After the panel, which lasted 45 minutes, the hotel hallway quickly clogged with caffeine addicts heading for the free coffee bar. I was sure my beloved wife would be bellying up for a re-buzz.

Eschewing that, I browsed a table loaded down with free (my favorite price) books and promotional gimmicks— including hardbacks and paperbacks, a deck of cards, a key chain, a small metal replica of a railroad spike, a bottle opener, three candy bars, and about a zillion bookmarks. I started stuffing giveaways into my conference swag bag. Just about everybody carried one of those bags, made of some cheap material and emblazoned with the QueenCon XI's fedora and trench coat logo.

"Hey, look at this!" Lynda suddenly appeared next to me, holding up a shot glass that I had somehow missed on the loot table. The gold flecks in her brown eyes shined more than usual. She had a cup of coffee in her other hand.

"Right up your alley," I observed, "you being a bourbon babe."

The red letters on the shot glass said **HOT SHOT**, with *A Jason Darke Thriller* below that. It was one of Seton's late novels, recently republished by Rue Morgue Books with a predictably lurid cover.

"Understated," she commented, "just like I'm sure his books are."

"I don't complain about the books you—"

The ringing of my smartphone interrupted this lie. Not that it really rang, of course. It erupted into the Indiana Jones theme song. A familiar face filled the screen, an elderly but ageless woman whose dyed hair looked pink. "It's Maggie," I informed Lynda, who used to be her boss at the *Erin Observer & News-Ledger*. I swiped the surface of the phone to answer.

"Hi, Maggie. What's up?" *As if I didn't know.*

"Sorry to bother you on a Saturday morning, Jeff. No rest for the wicked."

"Are you referring to you or me?"

She chuckled. "Both, I guess."

We always bantered like that. Maggie Barton has covered education, including St. Benignus University, for our hometown paper approximately since old St. Benignus ran the place himself. I exaggerate only slightly.

"I'm calling to see if you have a comment on a claim of police brutality made by a young woman named Lani Alvarez. I understand the ACLU may get involved in filing a lawsuit. Do you know about this?"

Lynda blew me a kiss and waved goodbye as she moved toward one of the rooms in which the panels were being held. *Coward!*

"It just so happens that I do. You're not the first person to brighten my morning with the news, Maggie. Let me assure you that St. Benignus University takes this accusation seriously, as we do all allegations about our employees. Officer Jackson has been placed on administrative leave, and the Erin police have been called in to do an independent investigation of what happened. We urge everyone to avoid a rush to judgement until all the facts are in."

Maggie had a few follow-up questions, which gave me the opportunity to defend both the free speech of the protestors and the tuition hike they were protesting against.

I felt like a juggler, not a new professional experience for me.

By the time I finished putting out that fire, Lynda and everybody else had dispersed to the panels of their choice. I slipped into one *not* of my choice, "Is the Golden Age All Mined Out?" I should have been at the only true crime element of the weekend, "Wrightsville Revisited: Big Crimes in Small Towns." In fact, I could have been one of the authors on the panel, based on my chronicles of Sebastian McCabe's exploits and escapades. But for personal and professional reasons, I went to the panel where Mac would be holding forth on a subject dear to his heart—the so-called Golden Age of mystery fiction.

You probably know that's a designation widely accorded the time between the two World Wars of the twentieth century. By extension, the term is often evoked when describing newer works characterized by clever puzzles and amateur or amateur-like detectives. So Mac is a Golden Age mystery writer in spirit, even though he was born in 1971.

As I sat down next to Lynda, the moderator was just finishing her introductions of panel members with ". . . McCabe, author of the Damon Devlin mysteries."

I whipped out my phone and took a picture of the aforementioned preening at the end of the table, to the right of newlywed Marcus Garber. Then I launched it into cyberspace via the St. Benignus twitter account with an accompanying descriptor: *Professor McCabe prepares to talk Golden Age at QueenCon mystery confab.*

That done, I turned my attention back to the moderator. She was what my southern-polite mother would have called a "solid woman" with ebony hair in a pageboy cut. Her glasses dangled over an ample bosom clad in a sweatshirt brandishing a logo of a black cat. I knew from a quick glance at the program on my way in that Callista

Jordache owned The Black Cat Bookstore in Winchester, Kentucky. Murder must advertise!

"One could fairly argue that, from a strictly literary point of view, the works of today's best mystery writers are far better than those of the Golden Age," she said in a deep voice—one that I had *not* heard the night before in the rotunda, it occurred to me. "They generally have more rounded characterization and richer thematic development.

"But that misses the point. The Golden Age has long been seen as an appropriate label for a heady time of great popularity and inventiveness for the genre. The crimes often seemed impossible and the killer was the least likely suspect. Mystery writers had their pictures on the cover of news magazines. Critics proposed rules for writing the detective story. Monsignor Knox even called them commandments. And people debated such precepts seriously.

"The Golden Age mystery at its height wasn't literature but a game—'the grandest game in the world,' John Dickson Carr famously called it. Later, some Golden Age writers became more interested in character and motivation as the detective novel evolved toward . . ."

While Jordache droned eruditely on, sounding more professorial than a professor, I scanned the program to see who shared the panel with Mac and Marcus Garber, creator of the sleuthing chef Pierre LeGrande. The other names weren't familiar to me, although they soon would be: Augustus Fitch, "chronicler of the Simon and Samantha Dale adventures;" Giles Hawthorne, "prolific British-born writer of horror, adventure, romance, science fiction, western, and mystery stories under fifteen pseudonyms;" and Letitia Crew, "a huge fan of Agatha Christie and author of the Crochet Club urban cozy series." *Urban cozy?*

With a long wind-up completed, the moderator finally threw her first pitch and I tuned back in.

"Ellery Queen, in whose name we are gathered this weekend, is today best known as the name of a mystery magazine, while Rex Stout, Agatha Christie, and Dorothy Sayers and their great detectives remain ever-popular. E-book editions of their books are flying off the virtual shelves. So what is the state of the Golden Age mystery today? And what of their successors in the field, those men and women who write in a style reminiscent of those days?"

Mac hopped on it, never mind that he was at the far end of the table from the moderator and the mobile microphone.

"Mystery subgenres wax and wane with the winds of fashion," he lectured, perhaps overdoing it on the alliteration. "Private eye novels, police procedurals, courtroom dramas, caper novels, and cozies have all had their day. And when that day was over, they all continued to have their devotees. So it is with the tale of the amateur sleuth, the first and therefore most venerable category of detective fiction."

No bias there.

"It all goes to story, not genres and the like," Giles Hawthorne put in crankily. Or was that Prince Charles? He sounded like the heir to the British throne, although he looked nothing like him. Hawthorne was pudgy, with a thick mop of salt and pepper hair hanging over his horn-rimmed glasses. He wore a corduroy jacket over a white shirt with button-down collar, no tie. "I've helped out a lot of writers who couldn't write in any genre, but they could tell a hell of a story. I won't name any, but one bloke's initials are R.C. And it doesn't matter what kind of label you put on it, or what planet it takes place on. The reader doesn't care and neither do publishers. A good story sells. That's why adults read Harry Potter, and not just fantasy fans."

Is this QueenCon or Comic-Con?

"You're spot-on about the meaninglessness of labels," Augustus Fitch agreed. The old gent looked like a product of the Golden Age himself, with white hair that was thin on top and long in the back. He had clear blue eyes and spoke deliberately, as if he didn't want to let go of a word until he was sure it was the right one. "We don't think of Dashiell Hammett as a Golden Age writer, and yet all of his work was done in the twenties and early thirties. Not only that, he created the first popular husband-and-wife team with Nick and Nora Charles as well as harder-boiled detectives. My Simon and Samantha Dale novels owe a lot to Hammett."

"I love Simon and Samantha," Lynda whispered, tickling my right ear in a most pleasant fashion. I liked the little squeeze she gave my hand, too. "But you can only read them as e-books."

Although I hadn't had that pleasure, Hammett I knew all about. *The Thin Man*, his last novel, set the standard for wealthy, witty couples drinking their way through to the solution of a crime. But *The Maltese Falcon*, featuring iconic private eye Sam Spade brought to life by Humphrey Bogart in the classic film version, is my favorite Hammett work.

"My guess," Fitch went on, "is that Golden Age stories, and their literary descendants today, appeal to people who are dissatisfied with the mess the world is in and are looking for an escape into a different time and a milieu untainted by realism. Isn't that why people still read Sherlock Holmes?" Mac looked as if he wanted to answer that, but Fitch didn't give him an opening. "I made a very deliberate decision to set the Simon and Samantha series in the early 1960s, before JFK was shot and the world went to hell in a handbasket. That's a nostalgic time for people who remember it, and even for some who don't."

"I remember the sixties," said Letitia Crew, "and so do my Crochet Club characters. Even though I was a little girl then, I knew that it was a very exciting and hopeful time amid the tumult of the marches and the sit-ins." Crew was a black woman with long gray hair, un-straightened, wearing wire-rimmed glasses. Mac told me later that she taught in the Department of English at the University of Notre Dame—or, rather, being a full professor with tenure, she didn't teach. "If I had put my characters in any time period other than now, whether in the so-called Golden Age or in the rebellious sixties, they would have to be very different kinds of stories."

"And perhaps not so cozy," Mac observed with a chuckle.

"Some people have compared cozies to romance novels"—*guilty!*—"but I think they're the direct descendant of Golden Age mysteries," Crew offered. "The big difference is that they are female-oriented in a way that even a feminist like Dorothy Sayers never pulled off in the twenties and thirties. Women mystery writers in those days mostly wrote about men. Think of Hercule Poirot and Lord Peter Wimsey." But I thought of Birdy Edwards and Melanie Swann's defense of her choice against a female PI. "Cozies are really about women. Men are just the sprinkles on the cupcake. But who doesn't love sprinkles?"

This woman lacked nothing in the assertiveness department. I tried to imagine her voice whispering, "*Where do we hide the body?*" It was no good. That wasn't the voice. Heck, the whole idea of a potential murderer among us was no good. Mac was probably right—isn't he usually? Lynda and I had just overheard a mystery writer in the early stages of plotting her next book. I reminded myself that a convention of mystery writers and fans is probably the last place on earth somebody would commit a real-life murder. That kind of thing only happens in mystery novels.

But wait—I could use that in a new and improved Max Cutter novel! Forget the idea of a campus protestor being murdered. I would probably have to make myself the killer anyway. Instead of that storyline, Max could appear at a mystery con to talk about what it's like to be a one-man-shop private investigator. And then somebody gets murdered. The contrast between Cutter, representing reality, and the mystery writers and their fans representing fantasy would be rich territory for thematic development, as Callista Jordache might put it.

Now all I needed was a victim, a killer, a motive, a title—stuff like that. A writer strongly resembling grumpy old Ned Seton would make a great victim, probably missed by nobody who knew him. But who would kill a man with one foot already in the grave? And I never based characters on real people anyway. In fact, one of the challenges of the book would be creating characters who *didn't* resemble real people in the world of mystery fiction. But I could do it!

And where would I put the body to add an extra element of drama?

All of this high-level thinking took just seconds to process.

"What about Miss Marple?" Marcus Garber wondered, back at the panel. "Wasn't she Golden Age?"

"She doesn't count," Letitia Crew informed him. "Christie made her so passive she was hardly a character at all."

Garber looked sheepish, if that's possible for a big guy with a shaved head. "I didn't even know about Golden Age until somebody used the phrase in an Amazon review of my first Pierre LeGrande book, *Cream of the Crime*. I mean, I never heard the term. I read a lot of mysteries, but I don't read much *about* mysteries. I guess what got me on this panel is that I especially love Nero Wolfe, so maybe my plots are a little Stout-esque. When I decided to write my first mystery I thought it would be fun to have a chef who solves a murder mystery. Fritz never got to do that for Wolfe, which is a shame."

After a little more back-and-forth among the panels, Jordache invited questions. When she called on someone, I looked behind me. It was the platinum blonde with the white eyepatch who'd been hanging on Rex Carter at the opening reception.

"I am wondering," she drawled in an accent redolent of black-eyed peas and boiled peanuts, "whether you see any echoes of the Golden Age in Rex Carter's Ian St. George series?" I'm told that there are traces of Virginia in my voice even today, after more than two decades in Ohio, but the south was thick as peanut butter in this woman's mouth.

Mac tackled that one. "In the earliest stories, St. George stands outside the law—or, rather, makes his own law. Such a character has always had a place in the mystery pantheon, even in the Golden Age. In particular, St. George bears more than a passing resemblance—"

At this point Lynda leaned over and mercifully distracted me with her nearness and the smell of her Cleopatra VII perfume. She slipped her Kindle Fire into my hands. I glanced down and saw that it was fired up to some deathless prose called *The Puzzle of the Soap Opera Slayer*. Less than riveted by Mac's lecture, I started reading.

"Colonel Mustard in the library with a revolver." Simon Dale spoke through clenched teeth while lighting a curved pipe that William Gillette had smoked on stage more than thirty years earlier.

"Sorry, Sherlock." His wife did not sound particularly sorry. "Wrong guess." She sipped a chilled martini.

Simon snorted. "I never guess." The editor of *Edgar Allan Poe Mystery Monthly*, who also wrote stories for the magazine under a handful of pseudonyms, applied all his considerable deductive skills to the game of Clue—but not always successfully.

So she has the revolver, he thought.

Samantha rolled the die. Four dots came up. "What's the big surprise for my birthday?"

"Just show up at eleven-thirty tomorrow morning at that address I gave you and you'll find out."

Instead of moving her piece—the red one—four spaces, Samantha leaned forward and gazed at her husband with the full force of her wide violet eyes. She had shifted into her seductive mode, refined to an art over the thirty-eight years of their marriage.

"It's not lunch at Twenty-One," she said in a low voice, as if to herself. "You wouldn't send me to that address. Is it a diamond?"

"Make your move, Sammie. Diamonds are for sixty. You were sixty *last* year." Samantha Dale was two years older and an inch taller than Simon. She'd had gray-white hair, undyed and cut short, for about thirty years. Simon thought it stunning.

Was this typical of indie writing? I wasn't sure, having never read any before. I handed Lynda back her e-reader. "Very interesting," I whispered diplomatically. *When do people whisper? When they don't want to be overheard.*

"Simon and Sammie are us in about twenty-five years," she assured me.

"I can't wait."

"Is that sarcasm?"

"I'm never sarcastic," I said with heavy irony.

Clapping alerted me that the panel was over. Lynda and I stood up.

She took back her Kindle and handed me a paperback book. "While you were taking your call before the panel, I picked this up for you off of the free table. Did you see it?"

The title over an image of a man's bloodstained body and a railroad track said *The End of the Line*. The subtitle announced that it was *A Birdy Edwards Mystery* by Melanie Swann.

"No, I missed it. But I'm very interested."

"I thought you would be—because of the train connection."

"Plus, the author was on the morning panel. I'll get her to sign it for me. Thanks!"

Lynda squeezed my hand. "I'm glad we came, Jeff. Isn't this a killer convention?"

She had no idea.

Chapter Six
No Ghosts Need Apply

Mac joined us for the luncheon event, which was to feature a Q&A with Rex Carter. It was held in the Taft Room on the second floor. All the major rooms at the Fountain Square Hotel are named after Ohio-born presidents. Maybe William Howard Taft got the biggest room because he was a Cincinnatian. Or maybe it's because he was the biggest president. He also had the coolest mustache, by the way.

"I trust your morning went well," my brother-in-law told Lynda and me as we sat down at one of the round tables dotting the chamber.

"Very immersive," I said. "Heck, I haven't even thought about what Maggie Barton's doing with that campus police brutality story." Lynda snorted. I pulled out my smartphone and looked up the *Online Observer*. No story yet.

"Plus"—I opened a can of Caffeine-Free Diet Coke—"I have a new favorite author named Melanie Swann." I looked around the room but didn't see her.

Mac raised an eyebrow. "You have read her work?"

"Almost. Lynda just gave me her latest."

"I should be very interested to get your reaction. She is generally considered an up-and-comer in the hard-boiled genre, and yet a discussion of her Birdy Edwards adventures would not have been out of place in the last panel. They are replete with such familiar Golden Age tropes as disguise, dying clues, exotic murder weapons, and locked-room murders. Ellery Queen and company would feel very much at home within those pages."

I wasn't sure how I felt about that, being generally not fond of such ploys.

"The panel on Queen and Sherlock Holmes made me want to read more EQ," Lynda said. "It sounds like the books changed a lot over the years."

Before Mac could launch an oration on that topic, a new voice entered the conversation.

"Is this seat available?"

"It awaits your presence!" Mac boomed.

I looked up and saw the long hair and sharp nose of Paul Malvern.

"You're Rex Carter's Boswell!" gushed a now-familiar woman with platinum hair and a white eyepatch. She was a bit wobbly on those red stiletto heels, which should have been registered with the police as lethal weapons. "I'm his biggest fan!" You could cut her accent with a chainsaw. *Ah'm his BIGGEST fan!*

"I know," Lynda muttered under her breath but next to my ear. Apparently she remained irked about this southern belle acing her out of a little conversation with Carter at the opening reception.

The fangirl stuck out her hand to Malvern. "Olympia Fail. I can't believe my luck meeting you. You must know everything about Rex." *Ah cain't believe mah luck.*

"Paul Malvern," he confirmed as he shook the proffered extremity. "Not everything, to be sure."

Mac initiated a round of self-introductions and more hand shaking. I tried not to stare at the eyepatch while I pressed the flesh with Ms. Fail.

"I've read all your books, Mr. McCabe," she assured him. "Yours, too, Mr. Cody." *Aw, shucks.* She focused on Mac. "You're like a real-life Ellery Queen—a mystery writer who's also a detective."

"One could say that," Mac admitted. "It would be equally accurate, however, to call Ellery Queen a fictional Edgar Allan Poe or Arthur Conan Doyle. Both of those writers were fair hands at solving crimes in real life. As for me, I have the advantage of a biographer who exaggerates my successes and ignores my failures."

I shrugged. *Who am I to argue with the truth?*

In short order we had taken our seats. Fail wound up with Mac on one side of her and Malvern on the other. Whether that made her a rose between two thorns, I wasn't ready to say. But it left her across the table from me, peering at my defanged Coke.

"Did you know that soda leaches the calcium out of your bones?" asked me.

Lynda guffawed. "I've been telling him that for years. He's in denial." *As if I would take health advice from you, my sweet. You used to smoke like a chimney in January!* But I made another mental note to take a daily calcium supplement just in case. I kept forgetting to do that.

I downed a defiant slug of the soft drink. Giving up on me, Olympia Fail turned her attention back to Malvern. "What's Rex Carter really like?"

Malvern appeared to think about that, as if he'd never been asked that question before—although I'm sure it's the standard query of anybody who knows a celebrity. Maybe the pause was just for show. "He's a complicated individual, but if I had to sum up his character in a word I would say 'tough.' I suppose 'stubborn' would work just as well. Cancer may kill him, but it won't defeat him."

Great line, I thought. Mac told me later that was a riff on a Hemingway quote, but Lynda had another take on it.

"Sounds a lot like Ian St. George, to me," she observed.

"There's certainly a lot of Rex in the character," Malvern said, "notably including a penchant for the extra-legal. I plan to explore that in the book, thanks to the statute of limitations."

"I hear he was quite the ladies' man in his day," Fail said. "That would be like St. George, too."

Malvern smiled. "My book won't be a tell-all on that subject, for the simple reason that he didn't tell me all and I didn't probe. It's not that kind of book. As I said, I don't know everything about him."

The talk went on like that for a while, the two St. George fans double-teaming Malvern with questions about their hero's creator and Mac occasionally offering commentary. That carried us through a lunch of citrus and basil marinated chicken breast drizzled with parmesan cream. Then the metaphorical curtain rose on Rex Carter seated on a chair at the front of the room facing a man I knew from the program to be Siegfried Van Cleef, veteran mystery critic for the *New York Gazette* and *Nero Wolfe Mystery Magazine*. Both men held microphones, a small round table between them holding glasses of (presumably) water.

Even from a distance I could once again see the effects of cancer and chemotherapy on Carter. Or maybe I was just remembering the gray and deeply lined skin from my closer view the night before. He looked like a man who'd rapidly lost weight, his clothes loose on him.

Van Cleef, by contrast, seemed the picture of health except for having a belly his suit coat didn't quite cover. He had a big head with fringes of hair on the side. I'd seen him at the reception the night before and thought of Alfred Hitchcock. His ponderous way of speaking into his microphone made me think he impressed himself.

"We are pleased to have with us today the leading representative, or perhaps the last survivor, of what might be called 'the gentleman thief school' of mystery fiction. Rex Carter has been writing about Ian St. George for more than forty years, although that may soon come to an end.

He has kindly agreed to answer a few questions this afternoon—first from me, and then from the audience. Would you like to start with a few words, Mr. Carter?"

The guest of honor smiled weakly. "It's a pleasure to be here," he said in an English accent with the edges worn off. "I think that's all I want to say to start."

"Right. Well, let's jump in, then. Critics less kind than I might say that the character St. George is a kind of pastiche of another Saint—Leslie Charteris's Simon Templar, branded as the Robin Hood of Modern Crime." This critique sounded vaguely familiar. "What do you say to that observation?"

"If I'm not mistaken, Siegfried, you *did* say exactly that in writing about a year ago when *A Dragon for St. George* came out. You didn't seem to like the book, either, as I recall."

Van Cleef's pause was a short one. "Well, let's say I hope your next will be better. But about my question—"

Carter shrugged. "That's an occupational hazard of the genre fiction writer. Every private eye is really pretty much like every other private eye in fiction, for example. Mike Hammer is Philip Marlowe with a quicker trigger finger and less subtle prose. So it's no surprise that one modern-day buccaneer would bear some resemblance to another. Of course Charteris was an influence on my early writing. And he, in turn, was influenced by Raffles and Arsène Lupin. And, come to that, did you ever count how many times the great Sherlock Holmes committed burglary?"

Van Cleef looked like he smelled something foul. "I can't say that I have."

"I think it's four."[5]

---

[5] The number of adventures in which Holmes engages in burglary—or something very like it—to retrieve something is actually five: "A Scandal in Bohemia," "The Adventure of Charles Augustus Milverton," "The Adventure of the Bruce-Partington Plans," "The Adventure of the

"But Holmes only acts outside the law in the name of justice."

"So does St. George—now. As my readers know, he's retired from what he used to call redistribution of wealth to himself. He has kept his ill-gotten gains but not added to them. However, he keeps getting himself into fixes where skills from his former life of crime come in handy to do things that the cops and other legal authorities can't, usually for political reasons."

"Political reasons like the Constitution of the United States, perhaps?"

That's when I thought: *Death of a Critic!* Some stuffed shirt like Van Cleef, but not *exactly* like Van Cleef, would make a great victim for my murder-at-the-mystery-con novel. Creating a cast of plausible suspects would be a snap.

Carter leaned forward with a death grip—excuse the expression—on his microphone. "I'm pretty sure I know the Constitution of this great country better than you do, Siegfried. I memorized the Bill of Rights when I became a U.S. citizen. I'm a fan of it, when correctly applied to protect the innocent and not criminals. But perhaps it has escaped your attention St. George (a) unlike me is a British subject, (b) operates around the world, often in countries with oppressive regimes where rights of any kind exist only on paper, if that, and (c) rather importantly, is a freaking fictional character."

His voice rose toward the end, but in a controlled way like a man just barely keeping a lid on it.

Not in the least displeased at this reaction, as demonstrated by the triumphant beam on his broad face, Van Cleef changed the subject.

"It's no secret that you're in poor health."

Illustrious Client," and "The Adventure of the Retired Colourman." Those are, alas, far from his only crimes. —Sebastian McCabe

Carter took a sip of water. Or was it gin or vodka? I gave it even odds. "Don't be so damned delicate, Van Cleef. I'm dying. I know that. Everybody knows that. I only hope my impending demise increases my book sales. That's the upside."

How's that for optimism?

"Thank you for a perfect segue to the question I wanted to ask. I'm sure you know that Sherlock Holmes, Nero Wolfe, Lord Peter Wimsey, and Hercule Poirot, along with many lesser lights, have continued on after the death of their creators in stories written by others. I wonder whether you would like to see Ian St. George continue on after your demise."

"Sure. I'd like to see him continue on in reprints of my books, and maybe a new TV series or a movie. But nobody else is going to write books about him until I'm long gone and the copyright on the character has expired."

Van Cleef raised his eyebrows in an almost comically exaggerated expression of surprise and doubt. Mac does it much better. "How can you be so sure?"

"My next book, *Murder, By George*, will put paid to the series."

"Is it true, then, that you're going to kill off the character?"

"No!" Olympia Fail 'whispered' so loudly that you probably heard it.

"More than that," Carter said. "I'm not just going to kill off the character. I'm going to kill his reputation so that nobody will want to bring him back. Who would want to write a Drury Lane pastiche?"

Van Cleef almost dropped his microphone. "You're saying that you plan to make St. George repugnant even to his fans, as he has long been to readers with more refined tastes? That's certainly an original goal for a series writer. How do you plan to accomplish it?"

"If you haven't figured it out already, buy a copy of *Murder, By George* and find out. My heirs will thank you."

"Won't St. George devotees feel cheated at this ignominious end to their hero?"

"They'll get over it. The earlier books still stand. As Pontius Pilate said, 'What I have written, I have written.'"

The Biblical reference made my head reel.

"You're confident, then, that you can finish the final installment of the series before you yourself are finished?" *Very delicately put, Van Cleef.*

"I already have. No ghost writer will be needed to complete Ian St. George's final adventure."

Chapter Seven
Fearing the Tin Man

Van Cleef jabbed at Carter for so long—never laying a glove on him, in my scoring—that there was no time for questions from the audience before the next panel.

"I have to talk to Rex," Olympia Fail announced to our table at large as the applause at the end of the slugfest died out. "Nice to meet you all." *Y'all.*

She rushed to the front of the room before her hero could escape.

"Carter was a fair-sized disappointment to this fan," Lynda told me. "Who do you think was the bigger a-hole—him or Van Cleef?"

"I vote for the critic, and I guess Ms. Fail would, too. She doesn't seem to be a bit turned off by Carter's not-so-winning personality. They're chatting merrily away up there. But then, she's such a St. George aficionado that she wears an eyepatch in homage. I wonder if she even really needs it."

"Wouldn't that be *aficionada* for a woman? But she's more like a groupie. Check out her body language—very flirty. And he's old enough to be her father!"

"Myself, I didn't warm up to him much," I said. "Even though Van Cleef was the ruder of the two, listening to Carter didn't make me want to start reading the St. George saga."

"Whether one should differentiate art from the artist is a classic debate," Mac informed us, not that anyone invited him into the conversation. "The late Mr. Francis

Albert Sinatra, for example, was without doubt an incomparable vocal artist. And yet I would not have chosen to fraternize with him and his associates after-hours in their notorious Las Vegas heyday."

I would have. But don't tell Lynda.

Shifting the topic to safer territory, I said, "What was that business about Drury Lane? Isn't that a theater in London?"

Mac nodded. "That it is, old boy, but not only that. Drury Lane is also the name of an amateur sleuth, a deaf actor, created by Manfred B. Lee and Frederic Dannay— better known as Ellery Queen—under the pseudonym of Barnaby Ross."

"Never heard of him."

"I think that was Carter's point, dear," my wife said helpfully.

"In the final Lane novel, aptly titled *Drury Lane's Last Case*—"

Spoiler alert! Skip the next paragraph if you don't want to find out why it was his last case.

"—the killer is Drury Lane himself, who then commits suicide at the end of the novel."

"Cheery," I quipped.

"So St. George is probably going to do something similar," Lynda speculated. "That's what Carter was hinting at. Once you're in the know, the title *Murder, By George* points to the 'surprise' ending like a giant arrow."

"Rex appears quite confident it is an ending that would forestall another writer from taking up his fallen banner after his demise," Mac noted. "However, that did not happen with another, much more famous detective who also became a murderer in his last adventure." *Spoiler alert! Etc.* "I refer, of course, to Hercule Poirot. He killed a killer and then succumbed to a failing heart in *Curtain*, a novel that was published just months before Agatha Christie's own death. I was most disappointed in the little man. And yet, the Poirot books kept selling and a new writer was authorized by the Christie estate a few years ago to carry on the series. So Rex's premise that Drury Lane's homicidal farewell doomed the character to obscurity fails to meet the smell test. The answer is much simpler than that: Unlike Poirot, Drury Lane simply was not a great creation."

"What I don't get," Lynda said, "is why the obvious title?"

"It's obvious because we know what it means, but maybe Carter thinks it's 'a little too obvious,' as Poe said somewhere," I speculated. "You know—the old double bluff, making the reader think it can't possibly be just what it looks like. Mystery writers do that all the time."

"Not Rex Carter," Mac informed me. "His *oeuvre* is not marked by that sort of Golden Age plot development, I assure you. I suggest that, despite his jocular comment about pleasing his heirs by buying his book, he is not much concerned about future sales at this point. He is dying and almost seems to take a nihilistic pleasure in it."

"But I still—"

"Mr. McCabe? Could you sign this book for me?" The interruption came from a thirty-something man in owlish glasses and a deerstalker cap. I'd noticed him the night before as part of a matched set, the other part being a female of similar age. He held out a copy of the latest Damon Devlin atrocity, *A Sleight Matter of Murder.* Why couldn't he wait until the mass book signing in the afternoon? I used to dream of impatient fans.

"I'd be delighted!" Mac assured him. "Your name, sir?"

"Toby Motherwell."

"What the hell?" Lynda muttered.

How uncharacteristic of Lynda to make a rude comment on a slightly unusual name, I thought—until I realized that her comment had nothing to do with the

Motherwell moniker. She was staring at her smartphone with a puzzled look on her beautiful oval face.

"What's up?"

She walked a few feet away from Mac and his acolyte, with me following like a well-trained pooch.

"It's a text from Megan Whitlock. She says some Austrian investor named Klaus Bonhaus has made a bid for the Grier Media Group's newspaper operations. You know a breakup of the company has been rumored for months. You even showed me that story in the *Wall Street Journal.* You're always reading that business stuff. Ever hear of this Bonhaus guy?"

"I'm afraid so. His last name is actually Habsburg-Bonhaus, but he downplays the first part of the surname."

Lynda wrinkled her brow. "Habsburg sounds familiar. Weren't the Habsburgs really rich and royal a long time ago, like centuries?"

"Right. And they're mostly still rich, although no longer royal. The Habsburgs of history were spread over several countries and ruled the Holy Roman Empire for about three hundred years, from the mid-fifteenth to the mid-eighteen centuries if I remember right." (I did.) "They stayed in the royal business on a smaller scale all the way into the twentieth century. Today a lot of the Habsburgs do charity and public service and such, but Klaus is in the business of buying and restructuring companies. He's sometimes known in the business press as the Tin Man."

"Why?"

"That's a matter of debate. Some people say it's because one of his first big deals involved making a lot of money on a tin mine that was supposed to have been played out until he licensed the technology to give it a new lease on life. Others say it's because he has no heart, like the Tin Man in *The Wizard of Oz.* He's made billions of euros and dollars in traditional industries by lopping jobs to boost the bottom line after he takes over. I don't think Habsburg-

Bonhaus has tried that in the newspaper business yet, but others have done it for years with a lot of financial success. I wouldn't say that the quality of American journalism has improved in the process, but you know more than I do about that."

"It's a mess. And this Austrian is going to do that to Grier? Holy shit! Pardon my French."

I was pretty sure that would be *Sacre Merde* in French, but I knew better than to say so. Lynda was in no mood for banter.

"Don't panic yet," I said.

"No? Then when *should* I panic?"

"Let's see what happens. The Grier board of directors may reject the offer. Or now that the newspapers are in play, a higher offer may come along from somebody with a different business plan. Or the government may not approve the deal." I didn't think the last was very likely. So far as I knew, the Tin Man didn't own any other newspaper operations in the United States that would cause anti-trust concerns. Plus, I couldn't think of the last time the Feds had put the kibosh on a big merger or acquisition. But it could happen this time, in theory.

"Wow, that's a long list of maybes! And one of those things could stop Habsburg-Bonhaus from getting his rich, formerly royal hands on the company?"

"Hey, if it were easy being a billionaire international tycoon, anybody could do it."

"You amaze me, Jeff."

This love patter undoubtedly would have continued apace were it not for a voice behind me—a voice I had heard once before in a whisper.

"This is the most fun I've ever had with my clothes on."

Not a very original line, I thought as I turned around to see who had spoken. She was a statuesque brunette with legs both long and shapely, not that I noticed. Before I had a chance to even read her nametag, she passed out of my sight in the crowded hallway.

"Wasn't that the voice we heard last night by the drinking fountain?" I asked Lynda. "I mean, I'm not imagining things, am I?"

"No way. That's definitely the voice we heard asking where to hide the body."

"Who Mac said was just plotting a mystery," I added. "Except that she was wearing a green nametag, meaning that she's a fan, not a writer."

Chapter Eight
Ice Cream Socialites

"You can ponder that during the next panel, *tesoro mio*."

If calling me her favorite pet name in Italian was Lynda's way of calming me down, it didn't work. But it did take my mind off of *dead* bodies.

That first panel of the afternoon caused Mac, Lynda, and me to go our separate ways. Mac went to "Sleuths and the Supernatural." Lynda was pumped about hearing Pandora Wheatley and Jade Delacorte hold forth on "Not Just for Laughs: Comic Characters in a Cozy."

"Reading cozies is just like eating popcorn, which everybody knows can be part of a healthy diet," Lynda assured me as she explained her choice.

Only if you don't load it up with salt and butter.

I'd have rather been taking a "Ride the Ducks" tour of the Ohio River—don't ask—than sit in on that panel. Fortunately, I didn't have to. Grant Pogue, one of the participants in that morning's session on private eyes, had donned his metaphorical judicial robes to moderate a panel on "Courtroom Capers: What Not to Do in a Legal Thriller." I don't read a lot of those, but the panelists entertained me with their different approaches to the subject.

Judge Pogue asserted that he would have found Perry Mason in contempt in every case. But Aristotle O'Doul, the most famous real-life defense attorney still in harness,[6] would have gone into partnership with Mason. Joe "Call me Z" Ziebart, police reporter for the online-only *Cincinnati Sentinel*, said he would have tried to get the fictional attorney to go on the record instead of dishing out the best stuff on background. Timyka Renfro, a thirtyish assistant prosecutor from Louisville, had never heard of Perry Mason but expressed chagrin that district attorneys almost never appear in mystery novels except as bunglers prosecuting the innocent.

When discussion on the stated topic of the panel began to lag, Ziebart grabbed the floor to complain that most fiction writers overlook the important role of the news media.

"What role—poisoning the jury pool by the presumption of guilt?" quipped O'Doul, looking at the journalist over his half-moon glasses. The veteran defender had more hair in his bushy eyebrows than in the gray fringes at the sides of his head, but he also sported a beard.

"The role of a free press in a democracy, where the public have a right to know, that's what role," Ziebart fired back. He somewhat undercut this flag-waving by scratching his head, where a mop of sandy hair was already in wild disarray. I'd heard of the *Sentinel*, his digital employer, but had never gone over the paywall to check it out.

"Before we get too far into the weeds here with mere real life, let's get back to fiction," Pogue suggested. "I wonder what you all think about how to make courtroom scenes more realistic."

"Don't do it," Ziebart advised. "If a novel read just like a trial transcript, it would be boring."

"Not in my cases," O'Doul said. "I see to that."

"Make the prosecution team more diverse," Renfro urged. "Prosecutors aren't all old white guys." She was

---

[6] See *No Police Like Holmes*, MX Publishing, 2011.

Exhibits A, B, and C of that because none of those three adjectives described her.

The shop talk continued for another half hour, with occasional sparks between Ziebart and one or the other of the legal lights on the panel to liven things up.

Then I went to the session on "How to Find an Agent" because I've never had one. One of the panelists, Harry Fingerman, dropped a few amusing anecdotes about what it was like to represent Rex Carter. That had me thinking that maybe I should get an agent and forget about going indie. From what I'd overheard here and there at QueenCon, there seemed to be a lot of dough in self-publishing—but also a lot of work. I wasn't sure I wanted to spend time and money formatting pages, getting covers designed and pages proofread, and so forth. If I was going to get back to writing fiction, I wanted to be a writer, not a publisher and editor. I left the panel with a lot of new ideas and decisions to be made ricocheting inside of my skull.

The break before the obviously-named Guest of Honor Event, featuring the unprecedented appearance of Rex Carter with Edward Seton, was accurately listed in the program as "Ice Cream Social." Several young servers dressed in white dished up cones of Graeter's for half an hour. Do you know how much sugar and calories were packed into each tasty bite of that stuff? I don't either, and I don't want to think about it.

People swarmed around the ice cream stations like flies on, well, ice cream. I stood back a bit and looked around for Lynda. But instead of seeing her, I spotted the brunette with the familiar voice getting a third scoop of chocolate ice cream piled onto a cone. She wore a pink blouse and a red bandana over a denim skirt, what there was of it. I casually made my way over to her, straining to read her nametag without being too obvious about it. I failed.

"Hi," she said, regarding me with wide blue eyes. I guess I'd gotten a little too close—close enough to catch her attention, anyway. I mumbled the same greeting back in the autopilot manner expected at such encounters.

"Flavor?" asked a young woman with a scoop in her hand.

"Um, vanilla." There's always vanilla.

"You're a writer, I see," the blue-eyed brunette commented with a warm smile that I would not immediately associate with a woman planning a murder. She put out her hand. "Avis Tiffin." This is known as networking.

"Jeff Cody. I've done a little true crime." No reaction, so she wasn't one of my readers. "I see by the color of your nametag that you're *not* a writer."

"Oh, but I am. Sort of. I mean, I hope to be." She began walking away to make room for others squeezing in to feed at the trough. I grabbed my cone, packed with vanilla ice cream, and followed. "My sister Bella and I are working on our first book now. We're going to use one pen name for the two of us, just like Ellery Queen. And the publisher could put just one photo on the back of the book, and it could represent both of us, see, because we're identical twins."

Cute. Very cute. She didn't seem lethal, I had to admit.

"I bet you have a great pen name."

Avis Tiffin shook her head mournfully. "Not yet. We can't agree on one we both like."

"How about 'Agatha Christie'? That should sell some books."

She giggled, just as she had at the reception. Or as her sister had; whatever.

"Hey, I think I heard you plotting your book at the reception last night. Something about hiding a body, wasn't it?"

She looked a little embarrassed maybe, but not guilty. "I'm afraid I got a little loud and Bella shushed me. Too much wine. Isn't that Giles Hawthorne?"

I looked behind me. The British writing machine, horn-rimmed glasses slightly askew, stood a few yards away on the other side of the ice cream stations in animated conversation with a tall, willowy woman with blond-gray hair. She seemed kind of faded out, her eyes a watery gray.

"Yeah, that's Hawthorne," I said. "I saw him on a panel this morning."

"Sorry I had to miss it. He's two of my favorite mystery writers, Jewel Hannaford and B.J. Sloan. Gosh, he's more than one person, and I'm only half of one, literarily speaking. Just think about that!"

No thanks, I'd rather not; it might hurt my head.

"I'm going to butt in," she added. "Excuse me."

Either Avis Tiffin's middle initials were A.D.H.D. or she wanted to get away from me and the perhaps-uncomfortable subject of hiding a body. I decided to hang with her and see if I could figure out which it was.

". . . was a low blow," I heard as I approached Hawthorne. This came from the woman with whom he was talking.

I didn't catch his response.

"Everybody in that panel knew you were talking about Rex Carter when you said his initials were R.C.," the woman retorted. I had a flashback to Hawthorne that morning at "Private Eyes and Other Tough Guys: *'I've helped out a lot of writers who couldn't write, but they could tell a hell of a story. I won't name any, but one bloke's initials are R.C.'*"

"And who are you to be critiquing his writing ability?" she raged on. "You're nothing but a hack under any of your pen names."

Hawthorne flinched as if he'd been hit, which I guess he had. "Well, that's your opinion of me, Ms. LeSourde. I can assure you that others differ, just as others differ with my opinion of Rex."

I gave him an A for effort, but the LeSourde woman cut him no slack.

"My husband never should have gotten involved with you."

Hawthorne unconsciously backed up an inch. "Eh? What's that? Who's your husband, then?"

"Rex Carter, you fool."

Chapter Nine
Signature Piece

"The whole exchange was more than a little tense," I told Lynda later.

"I guess so! Then what happened?" My wife, the journalist, loves a good story.

"Hawthorne may be a prolific wordsmith at the computer, but words failed him at that point. He just stared daggers at her and stalked away. And where were you? It's not like you to miss ice cream." That's why she joins me at the gym as many mornings as we can manage it.

"I was hanging out in a hallway with my phone. I called Megan to see what's going on with this Klaus Barbie guy."

"Klaus Bonhaus," I corrected. "So what's the story?"

"I think she was impressed by all those positive scenarios you gave me for what might happen next, but she doesn't know any more than she put in the text. It's all in flux right now. Then Mac's mom texted me a cute picture of Donata and we went back and forth for a while." She held up the phone and showed me said picture, which involved our daughter and cake in a messy embrace. As I looked, she went on: "So tell me more about this would-be writer who doesn't know where to hide the body."

I'd skimmed over my encounter with Avis Tiffin (no need to describe her legs) on my way to telling Lynda about Hawthorne's confrontation with Alison LeSourde, a.k.a. Mrs. Rex Carter.

"Her story seemed convincing enough, I guess," I conceded. "She's more like what my mother would call a flibbertigibbet than a homicidal type."

"There is no homicidal type."

"Fair point. Still, if I were writing a mystery novel, I'd make Ms. LeSourde the killer and Giles Hawthorne the victim."

"No you wouldn't, darling."

"I wouldn't?"

She shook her honey blond curls, which today were hanging loose. "Too obvious. They could work as decent red herrings, though."

Hey, who's the mystery writer here? I knew better than to ask.

This spousal chat took place in a corner of a third-floor room set aside for what the convention program unimaginatively called "Author Signings." This was a half-hour opportunity for readers to get their newly purchased (or otherwise) books signed by the authors. Not that every author at QueenCon took part; just the panelists. The room, named for Ulysses S. Grant, was conveniently located next door to the dealer room (Warren G. Harding), where books were available. Lynda had several in her arms.

"Rex Carter is getting a good crowd," she noted, changing the subject without warning. I'm used to that.

The authors sat at a long row of tables, two to a table. Carter, looking tired, nevertheless managed a smile and a few words with each book he signed. And he signed a lot, as Lynda had indicated. Paul Malvern, his biographer, sort of hovered in the background, but his wife stood beside him like a protective Mama Bear with her claws sheathed. I'd seen those claws in her set-to with Hawthorne. That prolific writer sat several tables over.

Several of the authors would be doing a reprise of sorts on the following Monday, signing their books at Mo's Mysteries & Marvels bookstore in Erin. I didn't know which ones, but probably not the top tier. The side trip to our town wouldn't generate enough sales to be worth it for somebody whose name had appeared on the *New York Times* best-seller list.

"I'm surprised Carter's one-woman fan club and her eyepatch aren't in line or hovering over him," I commented to Lynda. "She must have a bunch of books for him to sign."

"She probably already tackled him in the hallway between panels."

In contrast to the washed-out and weary Carter, Sebastian McCabe had never looked more exuberant. He sat greeting his fans two tables to the right of the dying man and on the other side of the none-too-spry Ned Seton. Traffic was brisk. I don't know what he was writing in all those books, but I can never break him of the execrable habit of inscribing my copies with the same quote from Sherlock Holmes—*"I am lost without my Boswell."* The joke grows stale.

Looking around, I saw a good percentage of the QueenCon attendees either signing books or getting them signed. Aristotle O'Doul, for example, was bent over at Grant Pogue's table getting the judge's scribble on a copy of *Quick and the Undead.*

The level of activity around each author was probably a good barometer of fame and sales. Lisa Ballantine was swamped, for example; Giles Hawthorne not so much. E-author Augustus Fitch, creator of that cozy 1960s rich couple with the sibilant names, had his share of fans asking him to sign Simon & Samantha bookmarks from their swag bags.

Lynda got in line to get some ink from Rex Carter, who, after all, was the lure that had brought us to QueenCon, even though she'd been disappointed by him at the luncheon. Mostly an e-book reader, she'd bought a copy of Carter's *Cat's-paw* in the room next door for signing. I'd already had Ned Seton sign *The Stainless Steel Trap*, and I also had *End Game*, but what the heck. I splurged on copies of his *Hugger-Mugger*, *Do or Die*, and *Fire and Ice*. He seemed to remember me, based on his comment, "Back for more?" But I noticed that he checked the name on my nametag before inscribing the paperbacks. He made each inscription slightly different, which showed that his creativity hadn't flagged any in his tenth decade.

The books signed, I glanced around the room. Melanie Swann looked lonely sitting right next to the popular Carter, with just her handbag for company. So I pulled out the copy of *The End of the Line* that Lynda had given me and presented it to her.

"Do you want me to inscribe it or just sign it?" she asked with a pro forma smile.

"Inscribe it, please."

Medium height for a woman, she peered up at me through her tangerine glasses at my nametag, which said **THOMAS Jefferson Cody**.

"I go by Jeff," I informed her helpfully. Never mind that Mac calls me "Jefferson" and Kate still sticks to "T.J." from our childhood. "I enjoyed the panel you were on this morning."

"Oh, thank you very much! That was fun. Have you read my other Birdy Edwards books?"

"That pleasure still awaits me." *Wait a minute – I sound like Mac! How did that happen?* "I love private eyes and I love trains, so I'm looking forward to this one."

"Enjoy."

She finished writing and handed the book back to me. "If you like it, the first is called *The Fat of the Land*." I told her I'd check it out and moved on.

A few feet away I opened the book and read, *"To Jeff, in the hope that this book will not be* The End of the Line *for you and Birdy Edwards. Melanie Swann 4/16/16."* I bet she said that to all the guys.

I looked up from the book and found myself face to face with a familiar pair of wide blue eyes. I stopped just short of walking into their owner.

"Ooops. Sorry." I almost added "Avis," but I quickly realized that it wasn't Avis, whom I thought of as "the rotunda whisperer." The nametag said **ARABELLA Tiffin**. This was Avis's twin, then—"Bella," her sister had called her—and identical she certainly was. Although now I realized that she was wearing dark slacks and her brunette hair was tied back instead of hanging loose.

"No problem."

Before I could formulate a way to ask her whether she and her sister had been plotting a mystery novel last night at the reception—not that I really doubted it—Arabella continued on and grabbed an autograph from Marcus Garber. I found out later that he drew little chef hats next to his signature, which his readers apparently thought adorable.

Just as I opened my swag bag to see if I had any more free books I could get inscribed, Lynda joined me with a health report:

"Rex Carter looks even worse close-up, poor man."

"His wife seemed very concerned, from what I observed. She didn't take her eyes off of him."

"Actually, I noticed she *did* look away from him a little bit while he was signing my book," Lynda recalled. "I could have sworn she was looking over at Seton, and not neutrally. There was some intense emotion there, but I couldn't tell what it was."

"Well, we know from Figg that Carter and Seton don't get along at all. I guess it's natural that Carter's wife would have some strong feelings about him as well. I told you how she tore into Hawthorne."

"Yeah, that makes sense. I'm sure that's it."

Chapter Ten
Figg Furioso

The Guest of Honor Event, billed as featuring Ned Seton answering questions from the crowd after an introduction by Rex Carter, was to be held in the McKinley Room half an hour after the book signings. Lynda, Mac, and I grabbed adjoining seats about fifteen minutes early.

By the 3:30 starting time the room had reached SRO status with no Seton or Carter in sight. About ten minutes later, with the natives restlessly checking their smartphones, Mac's mutton-chopped antagonist Lafcadio Figg finally rolled Seton into place in his wheelchair. Figg locked in the wheels with a jerk, as if he were in a hurry. It struck me how helpless Seton looked, his once hale-and-hearty figure now frail and totally dependent.

"Something is amiss," Mac announced.

"How do you figure that?"

"Lafcadio's irate body language and the expression on his face admit of no other interpretation. Choleric does not begin to describe him at the moment. A classic exhibition of Figg furioso! This does not bode well, Jefferson."

"And he's coming our way." By that I didn't just mean in our direction. He strode purposefully toward our row. Instinct told me that he was making a beeline for us.

"Perhaps he needs our assistance."

That'll be the day.

But he did.

"Have you seen Carter, any of you?" Figg demanded without preface. *Nice to see you, too.*

Mac arched an eyebrow. "You have misplaced the fellow, Lafcadio? That really is carrying the absent-minded professor trope a bit too far, don't you think?"

Figg just glowered, a homicidal look in his dark eyes.

Lynda held up her copy of *Cat's-paw*. "He signed my book."

"When?"

"Close to two-thirty, I guess, by the time I got through the line to him. But I didn't really notice."

Figg waved that away in a pompous hand gesture. "That was well over an hour ago. I had his assurance that he would meet me a few minutes before three-thirty in the lobby. I wanted to give him a few guidelines before he spoke to ensure that there would be no unpleasantness. He didn't show up and I haven't been able to reach him on the hotel phone or his cell phone. I've been searching the hotel for him, poking my head into conference rooms in case he got the wrong one."

"What about his wife?" I asked.

He shook his head. "I didn't see Alison, either."

"Well, there you have it," I said. "They're off somewhere having a romantic moment."

Lynda poked me in the ribs.

Mac stroked his beard. "I noticed Paul Malvern over there. Perhaps he—"

"I talked to him. He hasn't seen Carter since the book signing. Carter told him that he was going up to his room to rest. How long can a man rest?"

"Oh!" Lynda exclaimed. "Now I remember. I overheard Carter and LeSourde talking while I was waiting in line. Not that I was eavesdropping." *No journalist would ever do that!* "He said he needed to go to their room and take a nap as soon as the signing was finished at three o'clock.

She said she would go shopping at the Tiffany's across the street so she wouldn't disturb him."

This mollified Figg not in the least. "Why didn't he set an alarm? Or tell his wife when to come back? Of all the irresponsible . . ."

There was more, but you can fill in the blanks yourself. Figg stalked off toward the microphone at the front of the room to get the show on the road fifteen minutes late.

"He's not being very compassionate, considering the shape Carter is in," Lynda observed.

"And does that shock you?" Mac inquired. "Surely you know Lafcadio by now."

Wisely ignoring him, Lynda amplified. "Rex Carter is a very sick man. Something could have happened to him. Maybe Figg should be alerting the hotel management instead of dissing the poor guy."

Almost as if he had heard the critique, the aforementioned Figg put his wrath under wraps as he stood at a lectern and began his introduction on a mellow note:

"Welcome to the QueenCon XI Guest of Honor Event. My name is Lafcadio Figg, and I am a member of the host committee. Unfortunately, Rex Carter, who was scheduled to make the introduction of our honoree, was unavoidably detained this afternoon, so I will attempt to stand in the gap."

Olympia Fail sat in the second row, her good eye staring critically at Figg. I felt sure she regarded him as a poor substitute for the creator of Ian St. George.

"We are pleased this year to present the QueenCon Lifetime Achievement Award, colloquially known as the 'Queenie,' to Edward Seton." If there was any restraint in the applause on the part of sophisticates in the audience, I didn't detect it. "For more than thirty years, Ned Seton contributed his unique voice to the distinctly American subgenre of the private eye novel. Although all of his work appeared in paperback originals, generally an ephemeral form of fiction, discerning critics in recent years have lauded them for their rough poetry."

Rough poetry, eh? I suppose he meant Jason Darke lines like this typical passage from *The Stainless Steel Trap*:

> "Let's just say the people I work for, and you'd be surprised if I told you who they are, are like those three monkeys—see no evil, speak no evil, and hear no evil. You, Mr. Miller, are evil. And sometimes, so am I. My employers don't want to know what I do to get the results they want. That helps them to sleep at night, I guess. Myself, I sleep just fine. Are you comfortable? I didn't think so. You don't look like it. And we're just getting started."

Rough, yes; poetry, I'm not so sure.

The sound of clapping pulled me out of my literary reverie and alerted me that Figg had finished his introduction. He stepped away from the podium and handed a statue of Ellery Queen—the detective, not the two writers—to the wheelchair-bound writer. Seton sat up straighter in the chair to receive it. People all over the room snapped photos, some actually using cameras. When Seton then took the microphone from Figg, he seemed to shed about twenty years. His eyes lit up and his voice was strong.

"I never thought I'd get any awards," he said gruffly. Was that a slight catch I detected in his throat? "Hell, I was lucky to get paid. But I never got a royalty, you know. Gold Medal paid me, I forget how much—a few hundred bucks, maybe twelve hundred by the end—but it was a one-time payment for each book. That's why I wrote so many. Jason Darke was my best stuff. I wrote crap under other names, but Gold Medal bought that, too. People forget Gold Medal, but they published John D. MacDonald, Louis

L'Amour, and MacKinlay Kantor, so I was in good company."

He looked down at the statue in his hand. "Lifetime Achievement Award, eh? The only thing I don't like about it is the title. It sounds like I'm dead. Well, I'm not. And I figure I've got maybe one more good book in me, missing leg and all. It's been a long haul. I started writing right after I got out of the marines. There's no such thing as an ex-marine, you know. My pal Mickey Spillane's Mike Hammer novels were flying off the shelves back then, in the early '60s. The Mick was a good guy, even though he was Army Air Corps. He should have been a leatherneck.

"You know why I agreed to wheel myself here and accept this award? Two reasons: First of all, somebody asked me. I never got asked before." A mild collective chuckle rippled through the audience. "Secondly, I knew Fred Dannay, who was half of Ellery Queen. He bought a Jason Darke short story for *Ellery Queen's Mystery Magazine* when I really needed dough. He said it sucked but he bought it anyway. It was part of a special all-hardboiled issue, which also included a forgotten Sam Spade story and a new Lew Archer by Ross Macdonald. Maybe he thought I fit in. Or maybe he knew I wasn't doing so hot after Gold Medal folded. He was a nice guy, so maybe he wanted to help me out. I dunno."

Seton went along in that same garrulous fashion for some time, wandering from subject to subject about as aimlessly as a butterfly. He must have been a lonely man, and a disappointed one.

"I'm sorry that Rex Carter didn't make it here this afternoon," he said. "Or then again, maybe I'm not. When I heard he was going to say a few words about me, I wondered whether that kind of language is really allowed at QueenCon. I've known Carter for years. A lot of years. But I hadn't seen him in a long time until this weekend. And I'm still trying to work myself up to speaking to him again."

Half the crowd thought that was worth a nervous laugh, but not the half that included me. I got the impression that Seton was telling the truth like it was a lie, which is one of the best dodges in the mystery writer's bag of tricks. Figg stepped in before Seton could elaborate, which is sometimes another good ploy.

"I think it's time to invite questions from the audience," he announced.

Mac's formidable arm went up. Figg ignored him, pointing in turn to a succession of other curious souls with such questions as:

What's the future of the private eye story?

"That's like asking 'what's the future of the romance story or the western or the science fiction yarn.' Genres bounce around in popularity, up and down depending on the times. But a good writer can always break through. When that happens, the snobs say he 'transcends his genre,' whatever the hell that means. Not that anybody ever said that about me, so far as I know. Jason Darke is kind of *sui generis*, anyway. He's as much a private spy as a private eye because half the time he acts like a James Bond for hire."

Have you ever read a cozy?

"What's a cozy?"

(The questioner, an Amazonian woman dressed in an aqua pantsuit about a size too small, frowned and sat down. "That was Pandora Wheatley, author of *Tea and Cyanide*," Lynda informed me in an awed whisper. "The protagonist owns a tea shop and seven cats. She's been called the new Lilian Jackson Braun." I've never read the old one, who I'm sure was great.)

Who's your favorite living writer?

"Ned Seton."

Who's your favorite dead writer?

"Ned Seton. I like to think ahead."

What's your favorite of the books you've written?

"That's like asking me my favorite ex-wife. I love them all. Or at least I did at the time. But *Blood Moon* had the best ending. Look for the reprint later this year."

Finally, after a little more of that, Mac's persistent hand was the only one still raised. With a mixture of disgust and resignation on his face, Figg finally pointed at him.

"Yes, Sebastian?" He managed not to sigh. Mac addressed himself to Seton:

"As you noted in a previous answer, hard-boiled mystery fiction has waxed and waned in popularity. In my estimation, however, your work has never achieved the popularity or the critical acclaim that it deserves, unlike some others before and after you. How do you feel about that?"

Seton's well-aged face split into a grin. "I never cared, especially about the critics. I know what 'others' you're talking about—Hammett and Chandler and guys like that. James M. Cain. Critics treated them like they wrote literature, which they did. Even the Mick became almost respectable at the end. But you know what? They're dead and I'm still kicking at ninety-two, despite the cigarettes and booze." *But don't buy any green bananas, Ned.*

When the formidable figure of Siegfried Van Cleef rose from his seat, not bothering to put up his hand first, I knew the love-fest was over.

"Since you've mentioned your friend Mickey Spillane," he said, "I want to ask you about the close similarity between your *oeuvre* and his. One discerning critic called Jason Darke 'Mike Hammer without the charm.'"

Seton squinted. "Was that you who wrote that, Siggy?"

Members of the audience shifted uncomfortably in their seats in a kind of wave.

"No, Mr. Seton, that was Anthony Boucher, writing in the sixties, about a generation before my time. It is true, however, that I have also noted the derivative nature of your writing. The violence, the rough prose, and the comic book characterization so characteristic of Mr. Spillane are present in all of your works. And it is, indeed, hard to distinguish your ethically challenged protagonist from the symbolically named Mike Hammer."

You'd think Seton would be pounded into the floor by this, but he seemed rejuvenated by the joust.

"It's true that Hammer and Darke both took on the same kind of slime," he said. "By that I mean Nazis and Commies and people just as bad hiding under initials like KKK and SDS. But if there was any imitation involved between the Mick and me, you've got it backward. If you take a close look at his other character, the private spy Tiger Mann, you'll see that he bears more than a passing resemblance to Jason Darke."

"I'm aware of the Tiger Mann novels, but I have not had the pleasure of reading them." Van Cleef invested the word "pleasure" with Cody-level sarcasm. But he was a critic, so call it irony.

"You might like them, Siggy. You liked at least one Jason Darke story."

Van Cleef's body noticeably stiffened, as if the innocuous words had carried a sting. If Van Cleef wanted to respond to the dig, he never got a chance.

"And with that we're going to have to bring this panel to an end," Figg said quickly in his moderator voice. "I'm afraid we're already running a bit over on time." He hurriedly wrapped things up with the traditional thanks and a few reminders about the packed program for the day— one more panel, then dinner on our own, followed by the showing of an Ellery Queen TV show. Looking back at what was to come, I have no idea how it all fit into a single evening. You'll just have to trust me on that.

As we stood up, I noticed the willowy figure of Alison LeSourde rush to the front of the room and launch into an agitated discourse with Figg. Her body language told me that something was up, and it wasn't good. Before I had the chance to make that observation to Mac, he was already heading their way. Clearly, he intended to butt in and find out why Mrs. Carter was so vexed. Later on he claimed he acted in his capacity as a member of the QueenCon host committee, but I filed that under "Excuses." The McCabe curiosity had him on the move. Not feeling the need for an excuse, Lynda and I followed him.

To my surprise, Figg looked our way as if we were the rescuing cavalry. But he quickly focused back on LeSourde and kept talking. ". . . no idea, I assure you."

"Is there a problem?" Mac asked.

Carter's wife whirled around. "It's Rex. He's not in his room and he doesn't answer his cell. He was supposed to be here right now and he was looking forward to it. Something must have happened to him."

Chapter Eleven
Worst Fear Realized

"I certainly have no idea what the matter could be," Figg huffed defensively.

"Where do we hide the body?" I pushed that whispered memory aside, knowing that it had nothing to do with Rex Carter being AWOL. Did it?

"Did you check the hotel bar?" I asked.

Alison LeSourde gave me a frosty look with her watery gray eyes, as if I'd said something rude. "Rex is AA." *How was I supposed to know? And you should have looked there anyway.*

She appealed to Figg. "I'm very worried. Rex is so sick, and much frailer than you would think from the way he pushes himself. He could have taken a fall in some deserted nook or corner of the hotel."

"This fine old hostelry has an abundance of those," Mac noted.

"I understand your concern." Figg, ignoring Mac, was addressing LeSourde. "Perhaps my friends and I could divide up the hotel and take a discreet look around."

"That sounds kind of half-assed," Lynda said. "We have no special expertise in looking for lost mystery writers. Why don't you alert the hotel management and have them search, Lafcadio? Or if you really want to go all-out, have the moderators at the final panel spread the word that one of our authors is missing."

"That seems excessive at this point. Rex was last seen less than two hours ago. Let's not be driven by our fears. How often has your worst fear ever come to pass, Lynda? It doesn't seem wise to make a big fuss at this stage. I'm sure we don't want QueenCon XI to be remembered as the year of much ado about nothing."

Alison LeSourde's clenched fist told me she didn't much like Figg's reasoning. "You mean you don't want your little host committee to be embarrassed, isn't that it? That's what you're worried about – not what's happened to Rex!"

Mac cleared his throat, a sound roughly equivalent to a bull elephant in heat. "Perhaps Rex himself would be embarrassed if we were to make excessive commotion on his behalf. Most likely, as Lafcadio suggests, he is merely temporarily indisposed."

What's this—Mac and Figg on the same page? Alert the media!

Still not entirely convinced, LeSourde nevertheless agreed to let us try to find her husband. If that didn't work, she would call in the hotel management herself. I volunteered Lynda and myself to start at the lobby level, while Mac and Figg started on the fourth floor. We would meet somewhere in the middle. The guest rooms began on the fifth. LeSourde gave us her cell phone number before going back to her room in case Carter returned there.

"You seemed eager to take the lobby," Lynda commented as we took the elevator down. With the final QueenCon panel of the day underway and no other major convention in town, the elevator was deserted. "Do you think we'll find him reading the newspaper in one of those plush chairs down there?"

I shook my head. "The lobby level is where the bar is."

"But you heard his wife."

"Yeah, I heard her; I just don't agree with her premise that it's not even worth looking there. Alcoholics Anonymous does great work, but Carter wouldn't be the first member to have a relapse under pressure. Who knows what kind of strain he might be under, given his medical condition? He might just figure the hell with sobriety at this point in his waning life."

We got off the elevator, walked a few yards on plush carpeting, and found ourselves in Winston's, the watering hole attached to the hotel's Churchill Restaurant. I thought maybe they ran out of Ohio-born presidents after which to name public rooms. Later, though, I found out that the late British prime minister, and notable drinker, had visited the hotel shortly after its opening in the 1930s. His image was etched in the mirror over the bar.

Lynda looked at her watch, which was more jewelry than timepiece.

"I don't think we should order drinks," I said, "even if it is almost five o'clock."

"Of course not. We're on a mission here. I just want to keep track of the time."

Bellying up to the bar, we caught the attention of a young bartender with a mustache that W.H. Taft would have envied, complemented by a goatee that looked a bit like an exclamation point. After fending off his offer to set us up with libations, we established that he'd been there all afternoon.

"We're looking for a friend of ours," Lynda said. "He's in his late 60s, bald head, with wrinkly, gray skin."

"And a false mustache," I put in.

Mr. Taft looked at me as if he wondered whether our friend might find a blood transfusion more helpful than a drink. Or maybe he just thought we'd already spent too much time at another bar. It was hard to tell. "Doesn't sound familiar, and from that description I think I'd remember him. Afternoons aren't busy here, even on Saturdays."

We thanked him and left.

"That's that, then," Lynda said as she worked her smartphone with both thumbs. "Johanna's asking me what I know about Klaus Bonhaus." Johanna Rawls, "Tall Rawls" to me, is a good reporter at the *Erin Observer & News-Ledger* and Lynda's protégé of sorts. "The office must be in full panic mode."

"That's understandable," I said, "but maybe premature."

"And maybe not. That's what makes it so nerve-racking—the uncertainty."

My own nerves were a bit racked (or should that be "wracked"?) by this Carter-hunt because I didn't know what to make of it. Common sense and the law of averages said it was a waste of time, which almost guaranteed big trouble.

After I checked out the men's room in the lobby, we walked up the stairs to the mezzanine level. From there we looked back down at the lobby level, including Churchill's and Winston's just to make sure we hadn't missed anything. We hadn't, as far as I could tell. The mezzanine had a sales office, four board rooms, and a nineteenth-century French painting in a gilt frame, but no Rex Carter. Nobody else either, except for us. At past five in the afternoon—early for Winston's but apparently late for the mezzanine—all was quiet.

We walked up another half-floor to the second level, where Carter had held forth in the Taft Room. We arrived at the expansive foyer. Immediately to our left was a broad recessed area over which a lighted sign announced *MEN'S & LADIES' LOUNGES*. It wasn't a place you would go unless you had to go, if you know what I mean.

"I'll check out the men's loo," I announced, although I had no idea what would have brought Carter to this floor for a bathroom break.

"Since we're in the neighborhood, I'll powder my nose."

Inside the recessed area we had to go down another hallway to find the johns, which were right next to each other and appropriately labeled *MEN'S ROOM* and

WOMEN'S ROOM. What happened to the lounges? Lynda and I went into our respective rooms. All the stalls in mine were open, no Rex Carter in them, so I was out again in a flash.

Lynda wasn't.

I looked around, killing time, and noticed an alcove at the end of the hallway. Without much hope of success, I decided to check it out. Back in pre-cell days, that probably had been where one went to find a small bank of pay phones conveniently located near the restrooms. But now the alcove was almost empty.

Except for a body.

Crumpled on the thick carpet beneath an Italian marble ledge holding a vase of artificial flowers lay Rex Carter. A trail of drying blood streamed out of the side of his head.

Sometimes, Figg, your worst fear does come to pass.

As I knelt down for what I feared would be a fruitless attempt to find a pulse, I yelled for Lynda. It seemed like forever before she came out of the women's restroom. By that time I had confirmed the lack of life. But I was still huddled over the body, the angle such that Lynda couldn't see the blood from where she stood.

She gasped. "What the—"

"He's dead," I said.

Lynda shook her head sadly. "What a shame. He obviously thought he had more time."

"He should have had. He was murdered."

Chapter Twelve
The Big Why

Lynda called 911 and I called Mac. For once he was almost speechless, *almost* being the key word.

"The mind boggles," he muttered.

"What is it?" I could hear Figg ask. I hung up.

Mac and Figg showed up a few minutes later, hotel management in tow.

"Stay calm and stay here," said the agitated resident manager, a fiftyish man with a receding hairline and neat mustache. He looked like a floorwalker in a BBC sitcom. The metal nametag on his blue pinstriped suit announced that he was Brent Harrison.

"The police are on their way," added the guy from hotel security. "I called." He was a black man named Bill Crane, of average height and bigger than average muscle. Ex-military, I figured. "If the homicide captain comes, we go way back."

"I called them, too," Lynda said.

"Well," Harrison said.

"I don't suppose this happens often—murder in a hotel," Figg commented.

"Murder!" Harrison repeated.

"As Jefferson quickly observed, Rex clearly neither killed himself nor suffered a fatal accident," Mac said. "Nothing within sight could have inflicted that wound. The edge of the marble shelf is too rounded. It is also unbloodied."

Harrison looked horrified. "That's awful! Natural deaths and even suicides are an unavoidable reality in the hospitality field, but I've never worked at a hotel where someone was murdered."

Nobody's blaming you, Brent.

After a couple of minutes of this banter, the two hotel types moved off a few yards to confer between themselves. As soon as they did, Lynda verbalized the question that had been on my mind ever since we'd found Carter:

"Why would anybody take the risk of killing a man who was dying anyway?"

That's what I would call The Big Why.

Mac caressed his beard in thought, but kept any musings to himself.

"Dying?" Figg echoed, his portly chest stuck out in a futile effort to out-pompous Sebastian McCabe. "Half-dead is more like it. The time I spent with him and Alison yesterday before the reception left me seriously concerned about whether he was going to wake up this morning. He actually looked better today."

"He probably had good days and bad days," I platitudinized.

"The timing of natural death is never predictable," Mac noted. "My Uncle Boris was evicted from hospice after eighteen months of not dying, and then succumbed within a fortnight. So perhaps the killer was impatient, or more likely acted to assure that Rex would not have the chance to do something that he had planned to do."

"Such as?" Lynda prodded.

"No reader of mysteries, much less the writer of one, could fail to suggest the old time-honored convention of the change in the will."

Figg snorted. Even his muttonchops looked offended.

"All right, then, Lafcadio, how about this: A few fictional characters are fortunate enough to have truly passionate fans. Sherlock Holmes stands out, but not only him. Suppose an Ian St. George 'fangirl,' I believe the term is, took the extreme step of trying to save St. George from death in Rex's upcoming novel by killing Rex?"

Lynda gave him a hairy eyeball. "Why not a fanboy?"

"I have never heard the term."

And besides, I thought, we *know* he had a fangirl. I vividly remembered her strong reaction to the thought of St. George's demise.

"No matter," Figg announced, brushing Mac's possibly sexist verbiage aside. "This is absurd, Mac. The final St. George adventure, *Murder, By George*, is already written. And, surely, your highly speculative St. George fan would have been at the luncheon today and heard Rex say so, just as we did."

"But maybe the book hasn't been delivered to his agent or publisher yet," I said.

"That doesn't matter," Figg asserted. "The book is in his computer, and it won't be staying there. If anything, it's even more valuable as a posthumous work. I'm sure that Alison will make sure it sees the light of day."

"That's very rational, Lafcadio," Lynda said, "but anybody who would kill an author to save a character is a nutball anyway. So maybe rational doesn't matter in this business."

"I can think of another reason that might motivate an unstable person to murder a dying man," Mac said. "Or perhaps I should say two related reasons."

But I didn't let him say what they were. "Remember that whispered question, Mac? 'Where do we hide the body?' You said it must have been a mystery writer working out a plot."

"Of course I remember, old boy."

"I met the woman who said it and she's not a mystery writer, although she claims to be one in the making. Her name is Avis Tiffin."

"Avis!" Figg exploded. "I don't know what you're talking about, but Avis is—"

At that point Figg was interrupted by the rather noisy arrival of the cops. We didn't learn who Avis was until later.

Chapter Thirteen
Something Up His Sleeve

Investigating a homicide in Cincinnati is a much more labor-intensive affair than doing so in Erin, which has a police chief and a handful of officers.

First the street officers showed up. They called in a sergeant, who called in the lieutenant and the captain of the Cincinnati homicide unit. At every stage I got star treatment as the discoverer of the body. Mac, Figg, and Lynda verified my account as appropriate.

Before long the place was crawling with investigators and criminalists, those being their actual titles, supervised by the sergeant. I wrote all this down. The investigators conducted the interviews, starting with yours truly, and the criminalists collected blood, hair, and so forth, and photographed the body from all angles.

When the Captain showed up about an hour into the process, Mac greeted him like an old friend. It quickly became clear that was not exactly the case.

"Ricky!" Mac said.

"It's Dick," the Captain corrected in a grating voice that could have cracked glass. He stood about my height, with a wide face and big shoulders. He was in full uniform, including the white cap. You could tell he worked out, but he should have done more push-ups. "I've been called Dick for thirty years, McCabe." *I believe it.* "But you can call me Captain Kritzer."

"As you wish."

Oh, ho! What's this—another member of the Sebastian McCabe Unfan Club?

The smile on Figg's face might best be called wickedly beatific. He clearly enjoyed seeing his old frenemy bitch-slapped by the long (and brawny) arm of the law.

I didn't find out the backstory until later, and for all I know Figg never did. At that point all I knew about Kritzer was that he was giving Mac a hard look with a set of hazel eyes a movie star might die (or kill) for. Oh, and I also noticed that his hair was too black to be natural.

"In the circumstances, with the likelihood that this will be a high-profile case, I am quite surprised the chief is not on the scene," Mac said mildly.

Kritzer snorted. "He's on vacation, as usual." Since Erin is part of the Cincinnati TV market, I was aware of discontented murmurings that the bigger city's 68-year-old chief of police took too many days off and long lunches in between. "We don't need him. We don't need you, either, McCabe. I know you have a habit of sticking your nose into police business down in Erin, but that's not going to happen here."

"Of course not." Mac made it sound like the mere notion was absurd.

"Then go away while I talk to these subjects."

It took me a while to I figure out that he meant Lynda and me, we having been the "subjects" who found the body and called the police.

"What happened?" he asked. "I understand that you were actually looking for a body."

"Not a body," I corrected. "But we were looking for Rex Carter. Mac and Figg were, too. His wife asked us to."

I guess that didn't quite explain everything.

"Take it from the top. And take your time. Don't leave anything out."

So I went through it all again, from Figg having his shorts in a bunch because Rex Carter was nowhere to be found up to where I yelled for Lynda. Kritzer stopped me a few times to ask some clarifying questions.

"You didn't know Carter?"

"No."

"I've read all this books," Lynda put in.

Kritzer didn't even write that in his notebook.

"Carter's wife was worried about him because he was in poor health? That's why she sent you to look for him?"

"His health is more than just poor," I corrected. "It's no secret that he was terminal. Lung cancer."

With some apparent effort, Kritzer showed no reaction to that.

"You didn't move the body?"

"I know better than that."

"And the second floor was deserted when you showed up? Nobody coming or going?"

"Not that I saw."

"Nor I," Lynda added with grammatical precision.

"Okay." I thought that meant he was finished with us, but then he added, "Let's go back to the beginning, but this time try to estimate the times. I want to build a timetable."

This didn't take as long as it sounds. When we had given it our best shot, Kritzer thanked us and called Mac and Figg over for their turn. Actually, he just crooked a finger at them. As he did so, I checked my twitter feed out of nervous habit. @queenconxi had already tweeted: "*RIP Rex Carter. Sad to report mystery great died here at QCXI.*"

As a master tweeter myself, I had nothing but admiration for Figg's clear head in getting out the news so quickly. Also, he'd made great use of his time being kept on ice while Kritzer debriefed us. But now the Captain was ready for him and Mac.

Kritzer began with questions of timing, comparing their answers against the timetable. Then he shifted gears to,

"Why did Mr. and Mrs. Cody take the lower floors and you two the top?"

Why didn't you ask me that, Dick? Maybe he just thought of it.

"It was my idea," I interjected. "I wanted to look in the bar down in the lobby."

"Why?"

"Just a bright idea that didn't pan out. I've been to a few conventions, and I've noticed that the bars usually aren't deserted even during panels and business meetings. So I thought Carter might have been grabbing a quick refresher before the Guest of Honor Event and lost track of the time." In other words, I thought he might have fallen *way* off the wagon, but since I was wrong I didn't say so.

Kritzer went back over his notebook, underlined something, and then closed the cover. "I think that's it for now. The investigator has your room numbers and all of your contact information for when we need you again."

I didn't much like the sound of that "when."

"Anything else?"

I opened my mouth, but Mac spoke up first. "Motive is the sticking point, of course."

The Captain failed to repress a frown of annoyance. He must have been especially irked because he was too curious to just tell Mac to shut up. "Most murders are committed for money or sex and we know the identity of the killer within hours. That's been my experience over the past twenty-four years. Why should this be any different?"

"Because the victim was dying."

"So what? That wouldn't keep him from having a thousand dollars in his pocket that somebody wanted to liberate. This isn't a detective story, McCabe."

"Perhaps not." Mac made that sound like a big concession. "This hotel is, however, filled with mystery writers and aficionados who perhaps think differently than the average killer."

Kritzer would have been briefed about QueenCon, but he probably never thought about the implications until now. I could practically see the headache forming between his eyebrows and his suspiciously black hairline. "Define 'filled.' How many people are at this confab?"

"One hundred and seventy-eight," Figg supplied, "including fifty authors. I happen to know with some exactitude because I'm the chair of the local organizing committee for the con."

Bully for you!

"This isn't a secure area," Kritzer said, apparently to himself. "Anybody could walk in off the street. Still, I want a list of all the convention participants."

Figg nodded. "You will have it within minutes. I assure you of my full cooperation."

I bet. Figg, having noted the sparks flying between Mac and the homicide captain, would bend over backwards to help the latter. Besides, I'm sure he was thrilled to have such an important role in the investigation.

"Carter's wife is on the list—Alison LeSourde," he added.

"Okay, good. She can officially identify the body."

And also assume the role of chief suspect, motivated by either sex or money. That's a part tailor-made for spouses.

"Captain, there is one more thing I should tell you," I said.

"Oh? What's that?"

The tone of his voice indicated surprise that I had anything left to say, and rightly so. I should have brought this up earlier.

"Last night at the opening reception for QueenCon . . ." And I told him about the question that Lynda and I had overheard via the magic of the Union Terminal rotunda, Mac's assurance that this was merely mystery plotting in action, and my encounter earlier in the afternoon with the owner of that voice.

"She wasn't wearing a writer's nametag," I said, "but she claimed that she and her sister are working on a book. Maybe they are and maybe they aren't, but I thought you should know. Her name is Avis Tiffin."

"Well, that's interesting," Kritzer allowed in his glass-cutting voice.

"Avis is one of my most valuable volunteers," Figg said. "Didn't you notice her at the registration desk, Jeff?" *Uh, no.* He rolled on without waiting for an answer. "I started to tell you before. She's a Cincinnati resident who showed up a couple weeks ago and asked to help." That sounded suspect to me, a convenient appearance out of nowhere. "She's been handling all the social media for QueenCon."

"You mean social media like the announcement of Carter's death on Twitter?" I asked.

"Yes, of course."

"You didn't do it?"

He looked at me as if I had two heads, even though I was talking like I didn't even have one. "Isn't it clear that if Avis did it I didn't? Tweeting is not a two-person job."

"But how did she know about Carter?"

"From me, naturally. I dictated the wording to her as soon as I found out about Rex's demise from Sebastian." He turned to Kritzer. "And I'm sure you'll want to know, Captain, that Avis was with me the entire time from the end of the book-signing session until I went to meet Carter. Besides, she'd never met Carter. She told me so."

"That just happened to come up, the fact that she'd never met him?" Lynda asked skeptically. *Just what I was thinking.* How I love that woman!

"It came out in a conversation about the highlights of the con, as I recall. She was unfamiliar with Carter's work. I also know from previous discussions that Avis and her sister are, indeed, working on a mystery novel long-distance. The sister, Arabella, lives in Michigan, although she is here at QueenCon."

"We'll talk to both sisters," Kritzer said in a take-control tone of voice. "We'll talk to everybody."

"What about the murder weapon?" Mac prodded.

"Yeah, what about it?"

"I happened to glance at the body before you arrived." That my brother-in-law managed to say *happened* and *glance* with a straight face was a tribute to his acting prowess. "I noted the fatal wound in Rex's temple. Though I lack medical training, it was obvious that he was neither shot nor stabbed with a knife. The weapon must have been something out of the ordinary. Had you thought of a knitting needle? That would be more appropriate to use on an author of cozies, of course. However, if the killer—"

Sometimes even Sebastian McCabe knows when to apply the brakes. He did so, perhaps warned by the purple in Kritzer's face and the pulse throbbing in his thick neck.

"Let me warn you again, McCabe," he said slowly, with deadly deliberation. "I am in charge of this investigation. When I ask questions, you will answer them. Otherwise, keep your thoughts, speculations, fantasies, theories, opinions, and even questions to yourself. This is my town."

"Nobody steps on a church in my town." That's my favorite line from *Ghostbusters*, circa 1984, although I thought it wise to keep that to myself.

Mac arched his back and stood up to his full five-ten, which is fairly impressive given his excellent posture and his bulk.

"Very well. I assure you, Captain Kritzer, that I would never involve myself in a homicide investigation unless requested to do so by the local gendarmerie." Did Mac really believe that or did he plan to go to confession before Mass in the morning? "I give you my word that I will not so much as poke my perhaps overly-large proboscis into this affair without your approval."

"Which you won't get." Kritzer glared, probably just to keep in practice, and then added, "See that you don't."

"You no longer require our services?"

"You're a genius, McCabe." *Mac thinks so, too.* "Now beat it."

Mac bowed and strolled away, dignity intact, with Figg, Lynda, and I following.

I couldn't believe what I'd just observed—Sebastian McCabe promising not to get further involved in a murder case that had landed right at his feet. Mac's definition of the truth can be flexible at times, but it wasn't like him to break his word. He had to have something up his sleeve. Don't magicians always?

Chapter Fourteen
A Case for Cody & Cody

"Well, Sebastian, what do you think?" Figg asked as we headed to our rooms to drop off swag bags and get ready for dinner. Kate would be waiting for Mac in their suite down the hall from the room Lynda and I shared.

"I decline to speculate, Lafcadio. I promised as much to Captain Kritzer."

Not believing that for a second, I snorted.

"What's the deal between you two, anyway?" Lynda asked. "You and the Captain obviously have a history, Mac, and it's not a good one."

"Suffice it to say I know Captain Kritzer well enough to strongly suspect that he cheated on his police promotional exams to reach his current rank." *Ouch!*

"That's not why he loathes you," Figg stated.

"Loathe? Perhaps that is too strong a word." *No it isn't.* "Admittedly, however, there is a certain tension between Ricky and me. It dates back to a trivial matter from the mists of near-antiquity, namely the previous millennium. Surely this is no time to rake up those dead coals."

When Mac mixes metaphors, I know he's unnerved.

Lynda got a knowing look on her lovely face. "I bet it was a rivalry over a girl in high school."

"Our contentious past actually dates back to elementary school. More than that I do not care to say."

The four of us got in an elevator.

"Elementary, my dear McCabe?" Figg quipped.

As Mac opened his mouth to reply in kind—or, more likely, in *unkind*—the elevator doors opened on the fourth floor and Siegfried Van Cleef sailed in. I say sailed because that's how he moved, much more smoothly than you expect someone of his Hitchcockian figure to do.

"Oh, hello, there." His eyes swept the car until they landed on Figg. "Well, did you ever find Carter?"

The elevator doors shut and the car headed back up.

"Only his body," Mac said, never mind that Van Cleef hadn't addressed him.

"Eh? What do you mean?"

"I'm surprised it isn't all over the hotel by now," Figg said.

"The city, actually," Lynda said. "I, um, texted Morrie Kindle of the AP a while ago. I owe him a few favors." Based in Cincinnati, the Associated Press veteran has covered a number of stories in Erin over the years, usually ones that I wish nobody would cover. That's journalism for you. Still, we are telephone buddies and Facebook Friends.

"Texted him about what?" Van Cleef demanded, his feathers thoroughly ruffled. "What the hell are you people talking about?"

The elevator stopped at the seventh floor, which is where the Cody and McCabe rooms were located. I held the door open in a gentlemanly fashion to let Mac and Lynda get out first.

"Carter's dead," I said, serving it up plain before Mac or Figg had a chance to dress it up in a lot of multi-syllabic words. "Murdered. Enjoy your dinner."

The elevator doors closed on Van Cleef's shocked expression. Rather nice timing, I thought. Let Figg give him the rest of it.

"All right, Mac," I said. "Now that it's just us chickens, what's the gag? How could you give Kritzer your word that you wouldn't play Sherlock Holmes for the first time in your life?"

"Sherlock Holmes was a professional at his craft, the world's first unofficial consulting detective. I am a mere amateur, like Lord Peter Wimsey or Miss Marple."

"Don't play games with words," Lynda said. "Your promise was that you'd stay out of this case. But it's not in your DNA to just stand aside and let the experts do their jobs."

"I assure you that I intend to strictly honor my pledge."

"*Strictly?*" Only Jeff Cody could pack sarcasm, skepticism, and a demand for more information into one two-syllable word, if I do say so myself.

"Strictly, old boy! Quite strictly—for you will recall that I made no such promise about you two."

So that was it! Of all the screwy, ill-conceived, inconsiderate ideas that Sebastian McCabe had ever had in his arrogant, presumptuous—

Lynda took my arm. "We could do it, Jeff, you and I —just like Simon and Samantha Dale!"

"I will, of course, offer some helpful suggestions as to possible lines of inquiry," Mac said mildly.

"Of course," I fumed. "Suggestions. Listen, Mac, your pal Kritzer doesn't seem like the kind of guy to put up with any crap. And this is several kinds of crap. Not only are you splitting hairs over your so-called promise to the Captain, you're putting us in a position where we're bound to get crossways with him. Count me out. I'd like to have more children."

"I bet he just talks tough," Lynda said. "And can we not discuss this in the hallway?" As she spoke, she passed the plastic room key over the electronic reader and led us into the room where we were staying. It was large and elegant, with brocade curtains that made me want to look closely and see if Winston Churchill's cigar had left any burn holes.

Outnumbered two to one, I tried to even the odds. "Why don't we get Kate and deal her into this conversation? Isn't she waiting for you in your room, Mac?"

Lynda sat down on the king-sized bed. I joined her there (quit snickering), while Mac made himself at home in a chair big enough for even him to sit comfortably.

"Alas, Jefferson, your sister is not enthusiastic about my propensity to get involved in matters of a criminal nature. That is the real reason I gave my non-involvement pledge to Ricky Kritzer against all my instincts."

"You don't suppose that Kate being held hostage, kidnapped by that killer in London, had anything to do with her unreasonable attitude, do you?" I asked.[7] In the immediate aftermath of that frightening episode, Kate had seemed to shrug it off. But in the years since, she'd made enough cutting comments about it to make me wonder whether she continued to experience a mild form of delayed PTSD.

Mac waved my question away with an airy motion of his hand. Apparently to Sebastian McCabe that was water over the dam or under the bridge or wherever water goes. Sometimes I could just smack him.

"If this were an ordinary murder, I am sure the Cincinnati police could quite capably handle it despite the deficiencies of the captain in charge. However, I am convinced that the situation is extraordinary. Consider: A mystery writer known to be at death's door is murdered in a hotel full of mystery devotees. The notion that the killer will turn out to be his wife or a sneak thief simply strains credulity. That is too banal to be true.

"Therefore, I appeal to you. Will you be my agents in this?"

---

[7] See *The Disappearance of Mr. James Phillimore*, MX Publishing, 2013.

Agent sounded better than "Watson," I must admit. And getting involved in this screwy business, even as Mac's surrogates, would take Lynda's mind off her worries about the future of the Grier media empire and her place in it. But she answered Mac before I could, and it wasn't the answer I would have expected.

"First I want to know about you and Captain Shoulders," Lynda said. "Why are you two all Cain and Abel with each other?" She must have been reading the Bible again.

Mac sighed. "Very well, then, if you insist. It all goes back to an unfortunate incident in grammar school. Ricky and I attended St. Margaret of Scotland together here in Cincinnati before my family moved to Europe for my father's work at Procter & Gamble. In the seventh grade I was already practicing the noble craft of magic, but was understandably not as accomplished as I later became. During the lunch period one day, one of my tricks went awry."

"That doesn't sound so bad."

"If only the school administration shared your viewpoint, dear Lynda! My mishap resulted in Ricky's lunch bag being set on fire. We both received the same one-day suspension. That was rather unjust, I grant you, but punishing Ricky was not my idea. His parents sued the school to have the suspension removed from his school records. They lost and then lost again on appeal. By that time, fortunately, our family was living in Italy and I was able to avoid the Kritzer wrath for some years."

"That's kids' stuff," I protested. "Who nurses a seventh-grade grudge for thirty years?"

"Ricky Kritzer. He brings it up at every reunion. My multiple sincere apologies over the intervening years have been to no avail. To make matters worse, he quite irrationally blames me for his failure to get into St. Xavier High School and ultimately the University of Notre Dame."

"You'd better stay out of his way before he finds some excuse to throw you in the hoosegow," Lynda said. "Fortunately, you have us to help. Okay, let's work on suspects." She picked up a hotel-provided notepad and pen from the nightstand by the bed. "Who would kill Carter to keep him from publishing the final St. George novel?"

"His agent, Harry Fingerman, wouldn't like to see the gravy train chug to a halt," I suggested. "I saw him on a panel. So that's one suspect. And we've already talked about St. George fans." I had a mental image of the one-eyed Olympia Fail stabbing Carter in the temple with an ice pick, a crazed look on her face. It didn't seem so far-fetched.

Lynda wrote on her pad.

"As much as it pains me to concede this, Lafcadio had a valid point when he noted that Rex Carter's demise is unlikely to stop the publication of his last book," Mac said. "I would also stand by my contention earlier today that *Murder, By George* need not mean the end of St. George, as witnessed by the number of great characters who have long outlived their creators in the hands of other writers. Any devoted mystery reader would know that."

"But Carter made it clear that he didn't want that," I objected.

"His wishes became moot the moment he breathed his last. His literary estate could still authorize pastiches, as the Ian Fleming estate has done for decades."

"But if St. George dies in the last book, doesn't that put the kibosh on new adventures?" Lynda asked.

"By no means. You will recall that the real return of Sherlock Holmes was in *The Hound of the Baskervilles*, accomplished by the simple technique of setting the tale before the detective's supposed death. Later, of course, Dr. Watson and the rest of the world learned that Holmes was not really dead. Perhaps a new writer would find a clever way of doing the same for St. George. The death and resurrection of detective heroes—"

"Okay, we'll put the enraged fan hypothesis on hold," Lynda interrupted, "but I still think all these logical objections don't apply to a crazy person." With a sigh, she crossed out what she'd written on her pad. "So where does this leave us?"

"Alison LeSourde is a natural place to start," Mac said.

"Kritzer certainly will be giving her a hard look," I pointed out by way of agreement. "The spouse is always the first suspect. Why not kill him at home, you ask?" (Actually, nobody had asked.) "It would be kind of cute for her to do away with him some place far away from their domicile, namely here at the hotel during QueenCon, and then go crying to Figg about not knowing what happened to him."

"Motive?" Lynda asked.

I shrugged. "Maybe you'll get an idea when you talk to her."

"Thanks." The tone of her voice suggested that she found my comment unhelpful.

"Also talk to Harry Fingerman and Paul Malvern," Mac said. "They knew Carter well and may be able to propose suspects or lines of inquiry. Edward Seton is worth your attention as well. The antagonism between him and Carter is well known, and was even evinced by Seton today."

"But Seton is wheelchair-bound," I objected. "The only thing he's in any shape to kill is a bottle of bourbon."

A crafty look stole across Lynda's lovely face. "How do we know that? Maybe the wheelchair is a totally unnecessary fake-out to make it look like he couldn't have done it. Lots of one-legged people can walk with a prosthesis. This murder could have been long planned."

Mac clapped. "Brava, Lynda!"

"Okay," I said, a bit nettled that I hadn't thought of that, "if we're going that route we might as well do the third degree on Avis Tiffin, too."

Mac raised an eyebrow. "Lafcadio vouched for Ms. Tiffin, you will recall."

"Yeah, but who vouches for Figg? Maybe the two of them are in it together. If she lied about plotting a book with her sister, then maybe it was really Figg she was talking to at the Museum Center."

Even I didn't believe a word of that. But as a tabloid reporter once said, it *could* have happened.

"Lafcadio Figg as co-conspirator? What a delightful prospect, old boy! Have you any inkling as to a possible motive?"

"Sex or money, naturally. Or both—they say if you've got the money you can buy the sex." I was making this up on the fly, and not doing too badly at it.

"Well, I must acknowledge that theory is not beyond the bounds of all possibility, given the fallen nature of humanity." Mac stood up. "Tread down that path, then, if you feel so inclined. Do not, however, neglect the more likely avenues of inquiry. Please meet Kate and me for dinner at the Churchill at eight o'clock."

"What are you going to do meanwhile?" I asked.

"I am going to break the news to Kate that the game is afoot. Although my participation is relatively remote this time, she will not be pleased that murder has once again cast its grim shadow over our lives. I can only hope that a successful day of shopping has left her in a good mood."

Chapter Fifteen
Speaking Ill of the Dead

"So what now?" Lynda asked, looking down at her smartphone as we headed for the elevators.

"The last panel is over, so let's hit the lobby. I bet we run into somebody there who's on our list to grill."

"Won't people already be at dinner?"

"Not yet, at least not everybody. Some will be changing clothes first, or at least getting cleaned up, before getting together with friends for chow."

"Well, they'll have plenty to talk about at the table. Carter's demise has been posted on the QueenCon Facebook page. Same message as that tweet I saw earlier, but more words: 'We regret to report the unexpected passing this afternoon of Rex Carter here at QueenCon. We extend our sympathy to his wife, Alison LeSourde, and to all his family. He was part of our family, too. He will be missed."

Just once I'd like to read that a dead person will *not* be missed. Who missed Idi Amin, for instance?

"Ms. Tiffin's social media prowess has completely wiped out the element of surprise," I noted. "We can forget the old 'tell them about the murder and read the look on their faces' ploy."

"Oh, I don't know about that. Neither that post nor the tweet said it was murder. We can still try springing that angle."

Maybe it was my imagination, but when we got to the lobby level the place seemed to be buzzing with the news. It just seemed in the air as people with QueenCon nametags talked intensely to each other with serious looks on their faces.

"Rex Carter's fangirl, your pal Ms. Fail, is practically crying on Malvern's shoulder," Lynda pointed out, nodding toward the two of them standing by a potted palm.

"Is that what you call it," I snickered. He had his arm around her and she was looking up at him. At first I thought he'd grown, but then I realized she wasn't wearing her four-inch heels. Maybe that was an obscure mourning ritual. She looked like she'd been crying, and she held a crumpled tissue in her hands.

"If Malvern doesn't know more about Carter than anybody, except maybe his wife, then he's a pretty lame biographer," I told Lynda. "Let's interrupt."

We walked over to join the two Carterites.

"Such sad news about Rex Carter," Lynda said, by way of breaking the ice.

"Sad?" Fail repeated. The way she looked at me, kind of squinting, I had the impression she couldn't see well even in the eye without the patch. "It's devastating!"

"But hardly unexpected," I said. "His death, I mean."

She gave the tear glands and the tissue a workout. "How could he leave us so soon? We all knew he was sick, but we had such hopes that he would stay alive long enough to change his mind and give us more St. George adventures. Now we know for sure the next book is the last—no more St. George, no more Rex Carter. Paul just told me. I'm still trying to take it in."

It was interesting that she called him Paul, but people tend to get on a first-name basis rather quickly at conventions and conferences.

"It wasn't the cancer that got him," I announced. "He was murdered by a blow to the temple."

If they weren't both shocked, they were good actors.

"You're kidding!" Malvern said.

Fail stopped sniffing. "That's just crazy. Why the hell would anybody do a thing like that to such a wonderful man?"

"That's a really good question," Lynda said. "We were wondering ourselves. Especially since he was dying anyway. Who would profit from his death?"

Malvern wrinkled his brow. "You mean, like, financially?"

"In any way," I clarified.

Malvern shook his head, and his ponytail with it. "I think he was fairly well off, but I don't know anything about his will. That's hardly biography material. But since he was on the way out anyway, whomever benefits under the will didn't have long to wait."

Yes, yes, we've been over that.

I tried again. "What was the deal between Carter and Seton? Apparently they'd been feuding for years, but I never heard why. You must know."

"Yeah, I know." Malvern removed his arm from Fail's shoulder. "It's something I'll have to deal with in the book, so I guess there's no point in being coy about it. Carter stole Seton's wife years ago."

Fail gave him a reproachful look. "How can you steal a human being? A woman's not an object, like a diamond necklace or a bundle of cash. I'm sure she was a willing participant in being 'stolen.'"

"Ned didn't take it well, to understate the case," Malvern plunged on. "He made a lot of threats, leading to restraining orders. To tell you the truth, I don't know whether it was losing Alison that pissed him off or just losing."

"You mean Alison LeSourde?" Lynda clarified. "Carter's wife used to be Seton's wife?"

Malvern nodded. "His third and last. She was in her late thirties at the time they married, old enough to know better. Seton was just old, in his mid-seventies. It didn't last long. Alison must have been edging toward the door already when Rex came along. I've been working my way up to asking her about it for my book. There's a reason I'm thinking of calling it *Not Such a Saint: The Adventurous Life of Rex Carter*. Rex was pretty open with me about his love life, up to a point. I'm not sure how much I believe that he quit fooling around when he married Alison seventeen years ago."

"Once a rover . . ." Lynda sniffed.

Sex and money—those classic motives again, I reflected. And, as I'd proposed during the confab with Mac, it didn't have to be one or the other. Carter, at sixty-nine, had been only five or so years away from the age at which her previous husband had found himself sans Alison, if I had my math (92-17) right. Maybe she'd foolishly signed a pre-nuptial agreement that made divorce a less attractive prospect than homicide followed by inheritance. But there's still that pesky question: Why kill a walking dead man? *But wait!* Maybe Carter was the one who wanted out, and she needed to act before he could change the will. This had possibilities.

"What can you tell me about Alison LeSourde?" I said, after processing all of this in less time than it takes to tell.

"She wasn't that friendly to his greatest fans," Fail responded. "Overprotective, I'd call her. I mean, it's not like we were going to smother him to death with our reader love."

"Thanks for the view from your window," Lynda said, in a rather nice turn of phrase, "but I think Jeff was asking Mr. Malvern."

If looks could kill, Capt. Kritzer would have been called to the lobby in short order.

"Olympia's right," Malvern said. "Alison is—was—very protective of Rex. But it also went the other way. Rex worried a lot about her drinking. So much so that he recently convinced Alison to join AA. He's been on the wagon himself for years."

No wonder LeSourde had been so sure he wasn't hanging out in the bar.

"How did they meet?"

"Alison's an illustrator and she worked on an Ian St. George graphic novel. I think they actually met at a party in New York."

"Do you think they were happily married?" Lynda asked.

Malvern shrugged. "Who can really know? They seemed like it to me, but I've noticed that happily married people do unexpected things sometimes."

Was that a frown I detected beneath his companion's white eyepatch? How far had she gone in being a groupie?

"Why all the questions?" Malvern added, interrupting the questions I was asking myself.

"Just habit," I said. "I dabble in true crime writing, you know. But I guess you'll be cutting into my territory now. The life of Rex Carter has turned out to be murder mystery in the end. That should do wonders for sales of the authorized biography."

"My God, I didn't even think of that!"

Until then, neither had I. But it was something to consider – a motive for Paul Malvern.

Chapter Sixteen
Bar Talk

"Well, that was a good start," Lynda said as we walked away from our first interview.

"I'll say. I could write a soap opera based on the life of Rex Carter. If I were the suspicious sort, I'd be casting a long look at his widow." I outlined my thoughts on that.

"Too easy," Lynda offered. "How about Malvern did it to boost sales of his book?"

"That occurred to me. Pretty far-fetched, but the idea does have its charm."

We had talked our way to the entrance of the appropriately named Winston's bar.

"I bet some of the people we want to talk to are in here," Lynda said. "Let's go in and look around."

Translation: It's well past cocktail hour.

The place had filled up nicely, with a good portion of the clientele bearing QueenCon nametags.

"That's Harry Fingerman, Carter's agent, the snappy dresser in the three-piece suit over there at the table with Alexian Rowe and Aristotle O'Doul." I nodded in their direction.

"There's an empty chair for you, darling. And I can sit on your lap."

Appealing though that idea was, we wound up standing.

I approached the agent. "Mr. Fingerman? My name is Jeff Cody and this is my wife, Lynda. I saw you at the panel on agents this morning. I just want to say that I'm really sorry about Rex Carter. You must have been very close."

I stuck out my hand and he shook it solemnly.

"Thanks. I appreciate it. Rex and I were together a long time. Aren't you Sebastian McCabe's friend? I thought so. I've read your books. Very entertaining."

Well, at least Fingerman had good taste in literature! Also, his dignified manner impressed me, especially since I'd always thought of agents as one step below racing touts on the social scale. A handsome man with blondish hair going gray, he looked like he should be smoking a pipe. Instead, his right hand was occupied holding a cocktail glass in which a martini was keeping company with three large olives. The paper coaster on the table had a large *W* superimposed over a silhouette of the pub's namesake.

"I always loved the St. George books," Lynda said truthfully. "That's why we came to QueenCon."

"As a law-abiding officer of the court, I must strenuously condemn the character's crimes and vigilante actions," O'Doul said. "But I love them, too." His poison of choice looked like whiskey or whisky (the spelling varies), hold the rocks.

"The series has its fans," said Rowe, the book dealer, "and the early books in particular have a decent reputation. I've made a bit of money buying and selling St. George first editions at Crimes & Punishments. I even had Carter at the store for a book signing earlier this year, with Lisa Ballantine and a few other authors who happened to be in town at the same time."

It seemed to me that the book dealer had damned Carter with faint praise. I jumped on that.

"I gather that Ian St. George books aren't flying off the shelves these days," I said.

Fingerman beat Rowe to the answer:

"It's not like the glory days when the television series was must-see-TV for two glorious seasons in the nineties, but I have hopes for a revival."

Sparked perhaps by the author's splashy death? I filed that idea away for future consideration, which maybe shows how much the case had me floundering.

"I haven't got around to reading the books myself," I confessed, "but wasn't the most recent one, *A Dragon for St. George*, considered to be awful?"

"Yes," Rowe practically shouted. Maybe he should have stopped drinking one margarita earlier. "Some of my best customers complained to me about that damned *Dragon*, and even critics much kinder than Van Cleef agreed that it was the low point of the series. It pits St. George against a supervillain nicknamed—wait for it!—The Dragon, who turns out to be a Chinese woman funded by the government in Beijing. Dragon Lady, get it? And anybody who couldn't see that coming halfway through the book needs new glasses."

"I figured it out somewhere around page one hundred," Lynda informed him. "As a fan of the series, I have to admit I felt a little let down."

"You're being kind," Rowe said. "I bet you hated it. The best parts were only awful."

Fingerman winced. "That was totally my fault. I talked Rex into bringing in Hawthorne to ghost the book because he was having writer's block. I should have realized that all the perfumes of Arabia couldn't have made that stinker smell any better. The plot, which was all Rex's, was too implausible. Maybe it would have worked as a graphic novel, but not as a real book. Rex wouldn't admit that, though. He blamed Hawthorne for the novel's failure."

That must have been why Carter was so adamant that no ghostwriter would take over the series when he himself had become a ghost.

"So I guess he got his mojo back to write *Murder, By George*," Lynda said.

Rowe looked skeptical, but Fingerman nodded. "It's all his, and it's damned good. That's why I have hopes that it will revive the St. George brand. I might even be able to swing a deal for a new writer to take over the franchise."

"But Carter didn't want that. We heard him say so just hours ago, at lunch."

"That wasn't the first time I heard him say that, Lynda." See, conventioneers get on a first-name basis in no time. Nametags make it easy. "He was a very sick man and not thinking clearly when he came to that position. I'm sure that eventually I could have made him see that his heirs would benefit very nicely from new stories carefully edited for quality control by his literary executor."

"And who is that?" O'Doul asked.

"Alison—his wife. At any rate, there's no legal obstacle to stop the estate from authorizing new adventures of Ian St. George. We just need to figure out how to revive a character who's dead at the end of *Murder, By George*. We have options on ways to do that."

"What's the book like—other than apparently awesome?" I asked.

Fingerman's chuckle could only be characterized as wicked. "St. George settles some old scores in the course of the novel—and so does Rex. He knew it was going to be his last hurrah, so he used the opportunity to give the literary finger to a few people, so to speak."

"How so?"

"Readers who are in the know will recognize Giles Hawthorne, Ned Seton, and Siegfried Van Cleef among the characters in very thin disguise, heavily lampooned. Much of it is quite funny, although I don't expect the objects of his satire to find it so."

"I guess not," Rowe said. "None of the men you named is especially thick-skinned."

"Not to speak ill of the dead," Lynda said, "but I'm finding Rex Carter posthumously harder and harder to like."

"Don't be too tough on him," the agent said. "At least he didn't draw real blood. And, realistically, most readers won't even know who the characters in the book are in real life. Seton is still mostly forgotten, despite his recent revival, so the ex-marine who writes in a tortured prose about a Cold War private agent won't ring a lot of bells. Ditto in the case of Hawthorne, who mostly writes under various pseudonyms and the names of other writers. Van Cleef became Sigmund Van Winkle, a pompous fool who pays too much for trendy wines and reviews books he hasn't read. Rex's fellow mystery writers who have been scathed by Van Cleef will recognize the portrait—and there are plenty of those—but the ordinary reader will probably just see the character as comic relief."

When I was writing my Max Cutter novels, I never based a character on a real person. It was a matter of artistic pride with me. Also, I wasn't sure about libel law. "Wasn't Carter taking a legal risk? Not that he would be around for his day in court."

O'Doul looked bemused beneath his heavy eyebrows. "If you're thinking of defamation of character or something like that, I don't believe I've ever heard of a case involving a novel. It would be rather tricky. The plaintiff's attorney would have to prove that the negative fictional character was based on his client. So presumably he would have to show in court that the client had all of the negative attributes of the character."

He guffawed and took a slug of his drink of scotch, bourbon, or Irish whiskey. (Scotch would be my bet.)

Lynda's forehead wrinkled in thought. "Did Carter always put real people in his books? I never suspected it."

Fingerman shook his handsome head. "No, this book is special. Rex viewed it as payback time."

"On the one hand, you could certainly see why he was infuriated at Hawthorne," Rowe said. "But Carter also had an agent and a publisher. And he must have given final approval himself for the book to be published under his name. So there was plenty of blame to go around on the team. Right, Harry?"

The agent sipped his martini while he worked up a defense. "I guess we were all too eager to get a book out there," he said finally. "The e-book sales of the old titles were doing well and there hadn't been a new St. George in five years because of Rex's writer's block. But I'll take my share of the responsibility for that turkey. I blew it and so did the editor at Raven Books—and, yeah, so did Rex."

So Carter might have been justifiably upset with Fingerman and with his editor as well as with Hawthorne. Maybe they were all guest stars in the book. Even as I made a mental note of that, I wondered why I was doing so. Nobody would kill a man because of being parodied in a book. But the backstory—the slights and offenses that Carter tried to pay back in *Murder, By George*—could be motive-rich territory.

"His beef against Hawthorne was professional," I noted, "but with Seton it was personal. I'm curious: Did he have anything against Van Cleef other than a few bad reviews?"

"It wasn't just a few. Van Cleef has been disparaging his work ever since he landed the reviewing gig at the *New York Gazette* about twenty years ago. Rex seemed to think he had a particular animosity against him, but I've never believed that. Van Cleef has savaged lots of my clients." *Maybe that should tell you something, Harry.* "He's a nasty man with no real talent of his own."

"Who knew that Carter's final novel was a vehicle to skewer his least favorite people?" I asked.

Fingerman shrugged. "You got me. I didn't tell anybody, but Rex may have. Or Alison. Or somebody at

Raven. But nobody's said anything to me about it, so maybe the word isn't out there yet. Why do you ask, Jeff?"

"Nothing important. Just wondering who might want to inflict blunt force trauma on Rex Carter."

"I have no idea who the killer is, of course," O'Doul said, "but I'd love to defend him in court. The press coverage would be fantastic."

"Or her?" Lynda said.

"Or her. Sure."

O'Doul gave me his business card.

Chapter Seventeen
Cranky Old Man

"The way you phrased that was a kind of blunt force trauma in itself," Lynda said after we'd excused ourselves and moved on from Winston's.

We sat down in one of the plush leather sofas in the lobby and spoke in low tones.

"I was deliberately being harsh just to see if anybody winced," I explained.

"And?"

"They all did. Including you."

"Well, let's see what we got out of all that. O'Doul isn't in it at all, unless he's the least likely suspect in the best tradition of Agatha Christie. His only interest is the publicity he could get out of defending the killer. Right?"

"Right."

"And I don't suppose that Alexian Rowe killed Carter in revenge for *A Dragon for St. George*, which so dissatisfied some of his best customers."

"I don't find that too plausible, no."

"What about Harry Fingerman?"

"He doesn't profit from Carter's death in any way that we know. For some reason, Carter doesn't seem to have held that last book against him, and—"

"Wait a minute, darling. How do you know that?"

"He didn't replace him with another agent, did he?"

"Maybe he couldn't. If that book was such a drag on the market, maybe he couldn't get another agent. Or maybe he's locked into a multi-book contract."

"Okay, you win that one, Lyn, but it doesn't matter, does it? The fact remains that Fingerman was still Carter's agent and presumably would stay so as long as Carter lived. With Carter dead, the estate may give him the old heave-ho just on general principles. He couldn't be sure. Even if he was friendly with Alison while Carter was alive, that could change when the estate was in her hands. So I say that if Fingerman had a reason for killing Carter, it has to be something more important than what passes for job security in his business."

"What about Hawthorne?"

"Worth another look, even though it seems that Carter would have a better reason to kill *him*. Maybe Carter spread the word to his author pals in need of writing help that Hawthorne would screw up the narrative on the back of a cereal box. That could be deadly to his ghostwriting business."

Lynda looked skeptical with a capital S. "We haven't gotten a whiff of anything like that."

"True enough. Maybe that didn't happen. But those two certainly had a troubled relationship."

"Not as troubled as Van Cleef and Carter."

"Right again. Carter must have had dozens of reasons for wanting to snuff Van Cleef—every review that stuffed shirt ever wrote of a St. George book. You know, I'm not sure that Mac would be impressed by our progress. So far we're doing a great job of pinning murders that *didn't* happen on the one person to whom it *did* happen."

Lynda sat back, with a look of satisfaction on her face that I might have called smug on someone less adorable. "No, Carter didn't kill Van Cleef, but he did a literary hatchet job on him in his last book, no doubt thinking that turnabout was fair play. And Van Cleef could have found out about it from any number of people, according to what Fingerman said. My experience of critics is that they are some of the touchiest people on earth. They can dish it out, but they can't take it."

As the former editor of Henry Knox Wilcox's theatrical and book reviews for the *Erin Observer & News-Ledger*, Lynda spoke from experience.

"But Van Cleef would have to know that killing Carter wouldn't stop *Murder, By George* from being published," I pointed out.

"No, but it would be a strong form of revenge."

"The strongest! I'm not sure I can buy that motive, even for an obnoxious prig like Van Cleef."

After a moment's thought, I came up with an idea that, if it wasn't true, could be the basis of my Max Cutter novel-in-waiting.

"How about this: Suppose that in researching the book, Carter came up with some real dirt on Van Cleef— taking bribes for writing his rare good reviews, or something like that. And Van Cleef found out."

"That would work!"

But I felt myself frown. "Van Cleef did look surprised when we told him in the elevator that Carter was dead."

"Maybe he was just surprised that the body had been found so quickly or that we knew about it."

"Okay, put down Siegfried Van Cleef, the man with the poisoned pen, on your list as a definite maybe." I looked at the time on my smartphone. *Tempus* was *fugit*ing way too fast. "We're supposed to meet Mac and Kate for dinner in less than an hour. At this rate there won't be much to report. This is taking too long."

"Yep. I noticed that. I'm afraid we need to split up, *tesoro mio*. We can talk to twice as many people that way."

"Is that kosher?" I wasn't sure because the detectives I read about, being mostly private eyes, were lone eagles.

"Sleuthing pairs do it all the time, married or not. Steed and Mrs. Peel did it on *The Avengers*."

She had me there. We quickly agreed that I would talk to Ned Seton and she would handle Alison LeSourde.

"Figg should have their phone numbers from the conference registration forms," I said as I punched his name on the "Contacts" list in my phone.

I was half-right. He was able to give me a mobile number for Seton, but not for LeSourde. I didn't expect tracking down the widow to be a problem, though. Lynda would first try calling her room. If that failed, she would look around the hotel in the hope that LeSourde hadn't ventured out.

After a quick kiss, my bride went off to try to find out LeSourde's room number from Figg, who would know from having made the arrangements for the QueenCon headliners. I called Ned Seton.

"Seton speaking."

He could have said "growling" with more accuracy.

"Mr. Seton, this is Jeff Cody. We met last night at the reception when I had you sign a copy of *The Stainless Steel Trap* and then again this afternoon at the author signing."

"No refunds!"

I think he was kidding.

"I was wondering if I could talk to you for a few minutes."

"What about?"

Just wondering whether you murdered the current husband of your third wife, whom you may remember bearing some ill will.

"Rex Carter."

"That bastard! I'm the one who shouldn't have wanted to be seen with him, not the other way around. Figg was the one who had the brilliant idea to put us in the same room. Carter said he'd do it, then didn't show up. That's just bullshit."

What the hell! Seton was playing dumb about Carter's death. Or maybe not.

"He didn't stiff you." In retrospect, "stiff" was perhaps not the best word choice. "Rex Carter is dead."

"What! Already? I knew he was circling the drain, but not that fast."

"You didn't see it on Facebook?"

"I don't look at that crap."

Some days, I wish I didn't either. "This part isn't on Facebook yet, but he was murdered. Somebody jabbed something into his temple and left his body on the mezzanine level, where my wife and I found it."

"Well, I'll be a son of a bitch!"

You already are.

"So, can we talk, Mr. Seton?"

"Sure. I want to hear all the details. Come to my room, number eight-twenty-three. I'm having room service sent up. Going out to eat is more damned trouble than it's worth with this damned wheel chair." Actually, he didn't say damned either time, but my grandchildren may read this book someday.

When Seton opened the door of his room, I was surprised to find him leaning on a metal cane. He greeted me with, "You didn't happen to bring a flask, did you?"

"Sorry, no."

"I could sure use a drink. Sorry I can't offer you one. It was nice of you to come see me." He hobbled over to his wheelchair, which was parked between two double beds. I sat in a chair by a window with heavy curtains. "I wish I had a flask in this stupid cane, like St. George. That was one of the hokiest gimmicks in the whole hokey series."

"You read the books, then?"

Seton grunted. "I must be a masochist. But Rex and I go back a long way. We were never close, but we used to be friendly years ago. I want you to tell me everything about what happened to him."

"I don't know everything, but I'll tell you what I do know. When Carter didn't show up to introduce you, Figg was furious and Alison LeSourde was worried. So Figg and Mac—Sebastian McCabe—started looking for him on the fourth floor and my wife and I began with the lobby. We found his body a half-floor above where we started, in a deserted alcove where the pay phones used to be located."

"Already dead?"

At that inopportune moment the hotel phone rang. Seton didn't even look at it.

"Aren't you going to answer that?"

"No. If it's important, they'll call back. Was Rex already dead?"

"That's right. As I said, something had been shoved into his brain through the temple. We don't know what the something was because it wasn't left behind. Anyway, there was nothing for Lynda—my wife—and me to do but call nine-one-one and then Mac."

"The poor bastard." I assumed he meant Carter not Mac. "And I do mean bastard!"

"Paul Malvern told us that Alison LeSourde was married to you before she married Carter."

"I seem to recall that, yes."

Seton wasn't going out of his way to make this easy for me.

"At the risk of jumping to conclusions, I would guess that might be why you and Carter didn't get along."

Seton folded his hands in his lap. They trembled slightly. "There was a certain tension between us, you might say. Or there would have been if we ever saw each other."

"You saw each other today," I pointed out. "You were both at the author signing this afternoon."

"That's different. We didn't have to make nice. I was surprised as hell when Figg asked if he could have Rex introduce me at the guest of honor thing. But if there's anything I've learned in my long life, it's that life is full of surprises. I thought about it awhile and decided, what the hell—why not? All that crap with Rex and me and Alison was a long time ago."

I paused, trying to think of a diplomatic approach to what I wanted to ask. Then I had it:

"If Jason Darke were on this case, would he figure you for a good suspect?"

Seton threw back his head and laughed, not forced but a real laugh, revealing teeth much too perfect to be real. "That's good! That's really good, young man! McCabe wants you to ask me if I killed Rex." I was a little irked that he assumed I was there running an errand for Mac, and a lot irked that he assumed correctly. "From your description of the corpse, it sounds like the murderer got up close and personal with Rex and had at least a modicum of strength." He held out his hands. "Well, look at me. Do you think I could kill anybody without using a gun? I wish to God I could!"

"Point made, Mr. Seton."

"Ned."

"You may have to tell the police as well. They'll probably start by suspecting the victim's wife, and when they investigate her background they'll realize right away that some people would say you have good reason to hate her husband."

"But I don't! Hell, Alison and I were both better off after she left me." He leaned back in the wheelchair. "Not that I saw it that way at the time. She was the first woman who ever pulled the plug on me. And what a cliché, leaving me for a younger man! Rex had ten or twelve years on her, but he was a kid compared to me. But when I got over that I realized that we were never meant for the long haul,

Alison and me. I like my freedom. It took me three trips down the aisle to finally figure that out." Seton sighed. "But I have to admit, even at my age, I still get the old hankering once in a while to cozy up to something soft."

Try a plush toy, you old goat.

But wait! Maybe Seton had told me more than he intended. I tried to sound casual.

"So, have you scratched that itch lately—like maybe with your most recent ex-wife?" That would say something about her, although I wasn't sure what.

He shook his head, mournfully. "I wish I could. We had some good times back in the day. No, I hadn't even seen her in years until this weekend. I've heard about her here and there, but not too much."

"Like what? What have you heard?"

"Gossip says she has a bottle problem. I forget who told me. That's new since my time, if it's even true. I wouldn't know whether it's true or not. The closest I've come to Alison since she walked out on me was at the rotunda last night and again today at the book signing. She kept looking my way with a strange look on her face during the signing when she thought I wouldn't notice. I don't know what was on her mind, but it wasn't hanky-panky with yours truly."

"Maybe she was figuring out how to end Carter's suffering before he could change his will so that she's no longer his heir," I suggested. "That's an old chestnut, I know, but that doesn't mean it didn't happen."

For just a second the look on Seton's face gave me a peak at what he must have been like when he wasn't an old man in a wheelchair. And I was glad this wasn't then. I'm kind of allergic to pain.

"You're barking up the wrong tree, Sherlock."

"How do you know?"

"Because I know."

With a shock I realized that Edward Seton, creator of hard-boiled-twice-over Jason Darke, was a sentimentalist.

"Okay, then who would you pick as the one who saved Carter a trip to hospice? Who do you think had a good reason for killing a man well known for being *in extremis?*"

He didn't take a moment to think about it. "Siggy Van Cleef."

"Why?"

"Because he's a ruthless asshole. You saw what he did to me today. Was that any way to treat the guest of flipping honor?"

He didn't say "flipping."

"I'm afraid the Hamilton County prosecutor would need a little more than that to work with, Ned. I take it that he was less than charmed by your body of work?"

He waved that away. "That's nothing. Siggy doesn't like anybody except George Simenon and Rex Stout – maybe Patricia Highsmith if you get him on the right day. No, what bugged me was that the sniveling little worm slashed every one of my books that he bothered to notice at all, but my stuff was good enough for him to pirate."

"Pirate!" I had a sudden mental image of Van Cleef in an eyepatch.

"Hell, yes. And did you see how he flinched when I hit him back with it this afternoon?"

I accessed the Cody memory banks. What had been Seton's last comment to Van Cleef? *"You liked at least one Jason Darke story."* Whatever that meant.

"I didn't see his face, but I'd say from his body language that you hit the target. Figg obviously didn't want the audience to hear any more. What was that about? And what did you mean by calling Van Cleef a pirate?"

"What else would you call it? Not long ago he edited a collection of spy stories called *Spy vs. Spy*, a title that I'm pretty sure he ripped off of *Mad Magazine*. And he included in it the only Jason Darke short story, 'Darke of the Night.' I wrote it so long ago, in my early twenties, that I'd forgotten about it. It appeared in the last issue of *Rex Stout's Mystery Monthly* in 1947. I didn't start selling to Gold Medal for another five years."

"So he happened on your story and rescued it from obscurity. What's wrong with that?"

"Just a little thing called copyright. Van Cleef didn't get my permission or agree to pay me a royalty. He claimed it was a mistake, that he didn't realize the story was still under copyright. Hell, some of the later Sherlock Holmes stories are still copyright-protected in this country! There was a lawsuit over that not long ago. I keep up with this stuff. How could somebody in Van Cleef's position not know that U.S. copyright extends past the author's life? And I'm still kicking! I made sure he knew that!"

"Unpleasantness ensued?"

"Nothing his lawyer and my lawyer couldn't work out for a cash payment and an apology, but I made him sweat pretty good along the way."

"When exactly when was this?"

"Just last year, after I got 'rediscovered' by Malvern and my old stuff started getting a little buzz. So I'm thinking maybe Van Cleef did something even worse to Rex than he did to me, and Rex threatened to hit back hard."

I stood up. "Do you really believe that, Ned?"

Seton shrugged. "I guess it is pretty thin. I never spent a lot of time on trying to think up plausible plots. Neither did Shakespeare. But I know this: Van Cleef is a no-talent skunk. He wrote a couple of mysteries that went down like the *Titanic* so he's spent his whole career as a critic sniping at his betters. Tearing down doesn't take any talent at all. It's the story of every assassin of a great leader, the little man who takes down the big man – John Wilkes Booth, Lee Harvey Oswald, James Earl Ray. Why do they always have three names? But I'm rambling. Sorry. What are you going to do now?"

"Talk to a few more people."

The old writer hauled himself out of his wheelchair, leaning on the cane. "Do me a favor, will you? Tell Alison I'm truly sorry about Rex. I never hated him—or her—no matter what she thinks."

"I'll tell her if I see her."

As the door closed behind me, I heard the phone start ringing again. It didn't ring long.

Chapter Eighteen
Sorting Suspects

Mac, Kate, and Lynda were already into cocktails when I joined them late at the Churchill Restaurant.

"How were the stores?" I asked my sister.

"Great! I did most of my Christmas shopping."

It's April. By Christmas you won't remember where you put anything.

"I hope you were equally successful, Jefferson," Mac said. "Lynda has already filled us in on your discussion with Paul Malvern."

"But I didn't report yet on my solo efforts," she added. "I was saving that for you."

"Thanks. I had a nice chin-wag with Ned Seton. He makes a good argument that he didn't do it, and neither did Alison LeSourde, despite the love triangle that they formed with the victim. His favorite suspect is Siegfried Van Cleef." I sketched out Seton's beef with the critic.

"Rather amorphous in terms of motive, but not completely lacking in promise," Mac judged. "Perhaps you should speak with Mr. Van Cleef. I feel certain he will make an appearance at Lafcadio's hospitality suite later."

"I think the querulous critic would make a better victim than killer. At least in a book." *The Case of the Querulous Critic.* Not bad! "What he said to both Carter and Seton in public was over-the-top rude. If he does show up dead, check Olympia Fail's alibi."

"Those who can, do; those who can't, criticize," my sister said unoriginally.

"What's that supposed to mean?" I demanded.

Kate put down her amaretto sour. "Just that this Van Cleef person seems to be some big deal as a critic, but no great shakes as an anthologist. Maybe he muffed something else, something that Carter could hold over him or use to ruin him."

"Or maybe Seton only brought up Van Cleef to take the attention off of himself," Lynda said. "I was only able to stomach a few pages of a Jason Darke story, but that guy is harder than a diamond. I bet his creator is, too. And I further bet he wasn't as laid-back about his wife leaving him as he put on."

"But that was seventeen years ago!" I said.

"Some men are good brooders," Kate observed. Why was she looking at me?

"And besides," I added, "the poor man's in a wheelchair."

Mac peered over his mug of craft beer. "Not always, old boy."

"That's right, Jeff!" Lynda exclaimed. "You said he came to the door clutching a cane. Suppose it was a sword cane. Those aren't even hard to buy. I've seen them in stores."

"Seton would rather have a cane with a flask in it. I know that because he said so."

"Well, that means that the one he owns *doesn't* have a flask, so maybe it has a sword!"

I hated to burst Lynda's bubble—she's so darned cute when she's excited—but somebody had to do it. "Ned Seton may be able to move a few feet away from his wheelchair, but I'm pretty sure he isn't in sword-fighting condition."

That stopped her only long enough to enjoy a sip of her bourbon. "All right, then, suppose the murder weapon, whatever it was, was concealed one of the hollow metal arms of the wheelchair?"

Mac looked like he was supposing. "And how would a man in a wheelchair use this weapon?"

"Easy! First, he slips it out and puts it on his lap, maybe hiding it under a blanket or something. Then he asks Carter to bend down so that he can hear him better. Not suspecting anything, Carter complies. Seton whips out his weapon and rams it into his victim's temple. Carter is too surprised to do anything."

"Ingenious!" Mac muttered. "It is even possible."

"Very clever," I allowed. "Now, what did you get from Alison LeSourde?"

"You mean the graphic novel artist?" Kate asked.

I've known my sister all my life, she being about thirteen months closer to Social Security than me, but she still surprises me occasionally. "Do you know her?"

She shook her head. "No, we don't swim in the same artistic stream. But I recognize the name as being highly regarded in the field."

"If she's in her room, she's not answering the phone or the door," Lynda informed us. "So I wandered around the hotel a while but I didn't find her."

"That is regrettable," Mac said. "As the person presumably closest to the dead man, and probably Ricky Kritzer's chief suspect, her perspective is crucial."

"Too bad you aren't involved in the case, Sebastian," my sister said with a heavy dose of Cody sarcasm.

Mac turned to Lynda. "Well, what was your favorite part of QueenCon so far?"

Apparently she didn't realize that Mac was trying to move the subject matter into less dangerous waters. "Seeing Rex Carter—alive I mean, at the luncheon—even though he turned out to be not such a nice person. That's what I came here for, to see him before he passed. Who would have guessed that he was going to die so soon?"

Maybe not even the murderer, I thought. On the face of it, Carter's demise didn't look premeditated. Who would plan to kill somebody in a hotel alcove? But I didn't say that. I figured it was time to move on, following Mac's lead.

"I thought you would have said the coffee bar," I joshed. "But for me it was all downhill after the first panel, the private eye writers."

Lynda volleyed back that she adored the cozy panel that she went to, and Mac lauded the Golden Age one that he'd been on. We went on like that, sharing wisdom from various authors through dinner and dessert until almost 9:20. As we talked, I rubbernecked enough to spot Augustus Fitch, Melanie Swann, Grant Pogue, and several other familiar faces. In some cases, I suspected, authors were getting some grub with fortunate fans or aspiring writers. Marcus Garber and Lisa Ballantine, on the other hand, shared a table with their knot-tying rabbi, Brian Adelman. I hoped Garber liked the food, apparently being something of a gourmet.

"Professor McCabe?"

"Guilty, madam!"

The person who had addressed Mac thus was an Asian woman with chin-length black hair, equally black glasses, a tan vest, and a tweed cap. I bet she was thirty-one, even though her bangs made her look about half that.

"My name is Barbara Brant." She stuck out her hand. Although she spoke English approximately as well as I do and almost as well as Mac, there was something a little off in her pronunciation. I suspected a hint of Hong Kong. She continued talking as she shook Mac's hand first, and then the rest of ours. She sported aqua fingernails and a tattoo of a dragon with its head on her right hand and the body presumably running the length of her arm. "I'm a marketing consultant for the hotel. I also handle crisis communications, and Mr. Carter's murder has created a crisis." *Especially for Mr. Carter.* "May I sit down?"

"By all means."

She pulled over an empty chair.

"As you might imagine, a murder here is not the kind of attention any hotel wants. In this case in particular, it's not just the legacy media we're dealing with. Virtually all of the writers present at QueenCon XI tweet and blog and actively manage their Facebook pages, so this unfortunate situation has already gone viral."

"Of course," Mac said. "The victim took center stage at yesterday's luncheon. In addition, his work was well known to aficionados of action-based fiction, so there would be great interest in his demise beyond these walls."

"He will be missed," I added helpfully.

Brant nodded. "Yes, yes, I know all about Rex Carter. That's why Mr. Brent Harrison, the hotel manager, called me in so quickly. I, in turn, spoke with Mr. Lafcadio Figg, the chairman of the con. He's worried about the bad publicity for the event, naturally. He gave me your name as someone who might be of unique assistance. After Googling you, I can see why." Mac raised an eyebrow, probably surprised that anyone would need to run his name through a search engine. "You are a regular Sherlock Holmes, for sure! I should read your mysteries. If you solved the murder in quick time, that would become the big story. People would hardly notice where the murder took place." *A slight exaggeration, but I follow your PR logic.* "But Mr. Figg said you refuse to do it."

Mac's eyes slipped toward Kate, then gave Ms. Brant his full attention.

"Let us say, rather, that for more than one reason I have committed to distancing myself from the investigation of Mr. Carter's death."

"Mr. Figg said that maybe you were—how did he put it?—out of your depth on this one. But I'm hoping you will give it a shot anyway."

Mac raised an eyebrow.

"He said what?" Kate's question being rhetorical, she went on without waiting for an answer. "That weasel! Where would he have been if Mac hadn't cleared up that *1895* business?"

"Yes, well," Mac muttered. "That was some time ago and in another town. And do not forget that Captain Kritzer, as he prefers to be known, has discouraged my involvement in this matter." *Not to mention Kate doing likewise.*

"Did Figg know you were coming to make this request?" I asked Brant.

"Yes. I told him."

"Then I suspect he was baiting Professor McCabe with that 'out of his depth' business. He knew you would repeat it and he hoped that would get Mac off his duff and onto the case."

"So that he could solve it!"

"That would be the best outcome, sure – for Figg and for everybody but the murderer," I agreed. "But Figg also wouldn't mind too much if Mac fell on his face for a change. Either way, Figg wins. The only way he doesn't win is if Mac stays out."

"Or if Mac solves it," Lynda said, "which nobody really doubts that he could do."

"Wow!" Brant said, "That's deep! And I thought I was a strategic thinker!" She stood up. "If you can help the police, Professor McCabe, you would be irresponsible not to, whether they like it or not." She reached into a purse, pulled out a business card, and gave it to Mac. "Think about it, please. Call me if I can help."

She left.

"I bet she's good at what she does," I said. "How can you turn down a sweetheart like that, Mac?"

"She actually had a good point there at the end," Lynda said.

Kate looked at her as if she was giving that some thought.

The server returned our plastic cards and we realized that we'd better get moving if we were to make it to the final event of the day—the old Ellery Queen TV episode that was being shown in the Hayes Room.

We were just exiting Churchill's when I heard, "Hey! Lynda Teal!"

I knew that voice from the "Courtroom Capers" panel. The reporter with the sandy hair that looked like it had been combed by an eggbeater was ambling toward us, preceded by his paunch.

"Z!" my wife said. "I haven't seen you in ages." She announced all our names. "Joe Ziebart is the best crime reporter in town. He's been with the *Cincinnati Daily Times* forever."

"Not anymore," I said. "The *Cincinnati Sentinel*, right?"

"Right."

"I saw you on the panel this morning."

"I didn't know you'd jumped ship," Lynda said.

"Just started this week."

"Well, I hope it works out. The *Sentinel* is a brave effort at real journalism."

Ziebart shrugged off the compliment. "To tell you the truth, I didn't have much choice. I got caught in the latest round of layoffs at the *Times*, which seems to be going the way of most print products in this benighted age. The copy desk is gone and the photographers are supposed to write, too—blogs as well as stories for the paper. The whole news staff is down to about ten."

"I'd heard that, of course."

"Most of us who'd been around long enough to have experience and know the city are gone, along with enough Gen Xers to make it hard to prove age discrimination by the *Times*. A lot of us wound up on the *Sentinel*, along with a few refugees from TV news. It's a lean, mean, fighting machine, committed to living up to our name while traditional media continue to wither away."

That sounded like a mantra, a mission statement, and a call-to-arms all in one.

Lynda nodded sympathetically. "Journalism has changed so much just since I entered the field. It must be a sea change from when you started. Frankly, I don't know what's going to happen to Grier with this Austrian raider sniffing around."

"Speaking of which, I heard you went corporate. What are you doing at the crime scene?"

With that question, I realized that Ziebart was on the clock as a journalist. He must have picked up news of the murder from hotel buzz. Or maybe Morrie Kindle, alerted by Lynda, had already filed an Associated Press story.

"I'm not here on business, Z," Lynda said. "We just came for the convention."

Finding the body was a side benefit.

"Jefferson had the ill-luck of discovering the mortal remains of the late Rex Carter," Mac informed him.

Ziebart pulled out his notebook and started firing questions at Lynda and me. I saw no reason not to answer. I'm used to that in my day job. And Lynda would be ticked at me if I didn't. She still doesn't understand that freedom of the press doesn't override a private citizen's freedom to tell the press to take a hike if he or she is moved to do so.

The *Sentinel* man was good at asking questions, I'll give him that. *"Did you know it was Carter right away?" "Which temple—left or right?" "Describe the area where you found the body." "What time was this?" "Who did you call?"*

"Nine-one-one," Lynda said in answer to that last ungrammatical question.

"Mac," I replied at the same time.

Ziebart turned to Mac. "I know about you, of course. You've helped the police chief in Erin on—how many murders?"

"All too many, I am afraid."

"I'll second that," Kate put in.

Not to mention that mess in London.

Scribble, scribble. "So where are you on this case so far?"

"I am nowhere, Mr. Ziebart. I am quite sure that Captain Kritzer has the case well in hand."

And he even managed to not sound sarcastic.

Chapter Nineteen
Seeing Double

The evening's entertainment was the 49-minute "Adventure of the Pharaoh's Curse" from 1975, staring Jim Hutton as Ellery Queen. I missed it the first time around, so far as I know, being only one year old at the time.

"Previous QueenCons have shown episodes of the 1950s television series with Lee Bowman and the even older films with Ralph Bellamy and William Gargan as Ellery," Mac informed us on the way to the Hayes Room. "And one year we screened a made-for-TV movie with Peter Lawford. The Hutton series is a definite advance."

The plot—just to spare you from having to look it up on IMDB—is about a museum benefactor who dies in the museum of a heart attack. An Egyptologist shows up and blames a curse. But since this is a mystery, we know there has to be a human agent involved.

Near the end, Hutton, as Queen, breaks the "fourth wall" and talks to the viewers, telling us that we now have all the clues to solve the mystery. "This is a clever adaptation of the unique 'Challenge to the Reader' feature of the early Ellery Queen novels," Mac whispered. *Whatever.* The gimmick made me wonder whether Mac and Lynda and I knew everything we needed to know to put the finger on Carter's killer. Probably not, I decided, or Mac would have done it by now. Annoying he may be at times, but he *is* Sebastian McCabe.

The villain in the show—*spoiler alert!*—turns out to be a museum guard who tried to kill somebody in retribution for the death of the guard's son several years before.

"The revenge motif for an ancient injury is rather Doylean," Mac mused as we walked out of the room. "Numerous killers in Sherlock Holmes stories share that same motivation. I was about to say earlier this evening that revenge, perhaps combined with hatred, is the one reason I can think of to kill a dying man. The natural death of one's enemy might not bring sufficient satisfaction if the grievance were strong enough. A violent death at one's hands, however, most likely would do so—and Rex's murder was certainly violent."

Vengeance Is Mine was the name of an early Mike Hammer book. I filed that away and, I must admit, never thought about it again.

"Not that you have any interest in this case," Kate told her husband archly.

Mac bowed in her direction. "As you say."

Lynda ignored their byplay. "I was thinking along the revenge line myself. From what Fingerman said, *Murder, By George* is chock full of unflattering portraits of people Carter knew, thinly disguised. And apparently that was no big secret."

Mac stroked his beard. "That inevitably calls to mind a Sherlock Holmes story." *No kidding!* "'The Adventure of the Three Gables' revolves around a novel which is a *roman à clef* about the late author's relationship with a beautiful and wealthy widow who is willing to go to great lengths to suppress the manuscript. There is no murder in the story, however."

"Fascinating," I lied. "Hey, wait a minute. I see Avis Tiffin over there." We'd walked out of the Hayes room and now stood in the foyer. I nodded toward a mingling crowd several yards away that included Ms. Tiffin. "I can still practically hear her creepy, whispering voice asking her sister where to hide the body," I added. While that was true, I said it mostly to shut Mac up.

"Surely that has nothing to do with the murder of Rex Carter," Mac said. "One could hardly say that his mortal remains were hidden. The body was essentially out in the open, albeit in a part of the hotel receiving little traffic at the time—to say nothing of the fact that Lafcadio has provided Ms. Tiffin with an alibi."

The lady in question wore a dark blue dress with a scoop neck. Her sister, with identical brunette hair (although pulled back) and blue eyes, was still wearing the dark slacks I'd seen her in earlier in the day.

"There are two of them!" Lynda said.

"Twins," I agreed, "and about as identical as I've ever seen. The sister is named Arabella, Bella for short. I saw her having Marcus Garber sign a book for her this afternoon."

"Well, there goes her alibi."

"What do you mean?"

"Lafcadio said she was with him from the time Rex Carter was last seen until just before the Guest of Honor Event. But maybe it wasn't her! What else are twin sisters for but to provide fake alibis?"

I didn't think it would be a good idea for me to suggest that maybe Lynda reads too many detective stories. She's a piker at that compared to me, and I'm not even in the game compared to Mac. Besides, what respectable mystery writer today would use the twin alibi ploy? It must have been done some time, but not in a story I've ever read.

"I feel certain that Lafcadio is not so obtuse as to fail to see through such a substitution," Mac rumbled. "Identical though they might be, friends and family can usually tell twins apart."

"Not when they're trying to fool people," Lynda insisted. "I knew two girls in high school, the Keller twins, who fooled everybody for a whole day one April first, including their teachers and their boyfriends. One of the boyfriends claimed he knew all along, but neither girl believed him."

"But Bella wouldn't know things about QueenCon that Avis should have known," Kate said, seemingly drawn in despite herself.

"She would if she'd been fully briefed by her sister as part of a murder plot."

"How about motive?" If I hadn't asked, Mac would have. "It had to be more than just strong enough for Avis to take the risk of killing Carter—it had to be so strong that her sister agreed to help her do it."

"Do I have to do everything for you guys?" Lynda thought a moment. "Okay, how about this: Malvern more than hinted that Carter wasn't the most faithful of husbands. Suppose this person Avis and Carter had had what Mac would call a dalliance and she took it a lot more seriously than he did. Say he was ready to move on and she wasn't. Her sister, being her twin and close to her in all things, shared her anger. What do you think, Jeff?"

Sorry you asked. "Frankly, honey, the twin alibi thing is a bit hard to swallow, not to mention the fact that Carter hadn't been in any condition to be dallying for some time."

She frowned. "I thought you considered her a suspect."

"I didn't say that. I just said I couldn't get her voice out of my head."

"What do you think, Kate?" Lynda asked.

"I'm with Jeff to a point. Real-life murderers seldom go to great lengths to establish an alibi, from what I gather by reading. But Avis Tiffin is presumably somebody who thinks like a mystery writer, so real-life doesn't matter so much. And why are we talking about this since Mac promised not to get involved?"

I ignored the question. "Mac?"

"Highly improbable, I would say."

"Ah," Lynda said, "but all Sherlockians know that 'when you have eliminated the impossible, whatever remains, *however improbable*, must be the truth'!"

"Touché!" Mac lauded.

"But we haven't eliminated anything yet," I pointed out. "And anyway, Lyn, I thought you wanted to put the handcuffs on Ned Seton."

"He's still on my list. I'm keeping a wide-open mind. We haven't even talked to Carter's wife or Siegfried Van Cleef yet."

"The latter, never one to refuse free food and drink, is probably at Lafcadio's hospitality suite by now," Mac said. "I suggest that we join him and whoever else might be there, although I doubt that Alison LeSourde will be among the revelers."

Kate grabbed his arm. "Mac."

"Yes?"

"You promised."

"I assure you, my dear, that my interest is purely intellectual, a view from afar. Even Ricky Kritzer can hardly object if I ask a few questions or throw out a few theories. Everyone in Lafcadio's suite will be doing likewise, whether mystery writer or fan. That hardly constitutes involvement in the case."

But somehow I doubted that Capt. Kritzer would see it that way.

Chapter Twenty
A Ghost Speaks

If you've ever been to a confab, with the possible exception of one for the Women's Christian Temperance Union, you know that you can always find a hospitality suite just by following the noise. But things were relatively muted in room 944. I wouldn't want to be trying to sleep next door, mind you, but the death of Rex Carter had cast a certain pall over the festivities. By now everyone seemed to know that he hadn't succumbed to cancer.

"Maybe somebody got the brilliant idea to start killing mystery writers, like it's a big joke," was the first thing we heard as we neared the open door of the suite. I recognized that voice—Avis Tiffin. Mac looked at me with a raised eyebrow.

We walked into a party that felt like a wake, but not an Irish one.

"Don't be silly," retorted Melanie Swann, who looked like a writer of cozies and talked like John D. MacDonald after a hard day at the office. I didn't know yet how she wrote. "Nobody would be that corny."

"It does seem a little fanciful, not to mention premature, to speculate along those lines," Lafcadio Figg agreed. "There has only been one murder, thank God."

"So far as we know."

"And no reason to believe there will be any more," Figg added almost before Swann had finished her clarifying sentence.

"I'm not worried," offered Avis Tiffin, standing next to her doppelgänger and a blond-haired man. Well, why would *she* worry? Throwing around a few ideas for a plot with her sister hardly qualified her as a mystery writer. Or was she trying to establish herself as one by asking the question? And if so, did she have a reason for doing that? These altogether too-convoluted thoughts ran through my head as she added: "If the cops can't figure it out, I'm sure one of the fictional detectives represented here could."

"Kritzer would love to hear that," I murmured in Lynda's ear.

"It would be a natural case for Simon and Samantha Dale," announced the elderly Augustus Fitch, looking a little worn-out at the end of a long day. His baby blues seemed big behind his glasses. He clutched a glass of bourbon in his hand like he was afraid it was going to escape from him. "As the editor of a mystery magazine, Simon probably would have bought stories from Rex Carter. Several of the St. George books were collections of novellas that appeared first in periodicals."

"So how would the Dales solve the case?" Lynda asked.

"Oh, the usual. They would ask a lot of questions in their own charming way. Everybody would lie to them because they all have secrets of a romantic or financial nature to protect. But Sammie would wake up in the middle of the night and remember the killer's self-contradicting lie that opens the flood-gates for Simon to figure out the rest."

Oh.

"No offense," Lisa Ballantine said, "but this being real life, I'm sure the Cincinnati police don't need any amateur help to solve Rex's murder. I wonder if they would let me watch? That would be cool. The LAPD has always been very helpful to me when I'm researching my Kim Braxton novels."

Mac regarded the petite blonde. "I would not count on it. Helpful is not a word that I would typically associate with Captain Kritzer."

"I'll turn on the charm."

"That won't help," I assured her.

"Then I'll offer to be interviewed. I don't know anything, of course, but the cops won't know that until they talk to me. I really want to see how the police operate in a medium-sized city."

"I'm sure Cincinnati's Finest are quite capable," said Marcus Garber, AKA the newly minted Mr. Lisa Ballantine. "But this isn't your garden-variety mystery."

"Like maybe it would take a baker to solve it?" his wife said.

Ouch!

"No, dear, I was thinking it might take a mystery writer to solve the murder of a mystery writer, somebody who can think outside the box."

Since "think outside the box" has become a cliché, I always figure anybody who says "think outside the box" is not thinking outside the box.

"Fat chance," his wife shot back. *I hope there's a couch in the honeymoon suite.* But somehow I had a feeling that this difference of opinion among the honeymooners about the merits of their respective subgenres had been aired before. Maybe they belonged to different political parties, too. Opposites attract and all that. Love is one of the greatest mysteries. Lani Alvarez had dated a campus cop, although maybe that's a poor example.

"You must concede, Ms. Ballantine, that the successful amateur sleuth is not entirely the province of fiction," Mac observed mildly. "Arthur Conan Doyle was involved in the solution of several real-life crimes. In particular, he is well known for vindicating two men wrongly accused. I myself have been of help to the legal authorities in several cases."

"Weren't those cases of yours in a very small Ohio town with a small police force?" Ballantine asked.

"One was in London," Kate asserted. "And he helped Scotland Yard." That was also the business in which she'd been taken hostage, but Kate apparently put her PTSD on hold under the circumstances: Her man was under attack.

"Still," Ballantine said, "my money is on the local police and I'd like to watch them do it."

"This conversation makes me curious," Fitch announced. He addressed Mac: "How does the way you approach a case compare to the way your sleuth would do it?"

Mac displayed no faux reluctance to hold forth.

"There is very little difference. The solution to a Damon Devlin mystery often depends on motive, which is of great interest to me in real life as well. Why anyone would kill Rex Carter is a particularly intriguing element in this instance because it was well known that he was dying anyway. At the moment, then, the motive remains obscure.

"Motive aside, sifting through alibis is an efficient way to reduce the pool of potential suspects. That would be especially helpful in this situation, where there are so many suspects. So Damon Devlin might even ask you, Ms. Tiffin, where were you yesterday from the end of the book signing to the beginning of the Guest of Honor Event?"

"I told you—" Figg began.

"I was with him, like his shadow." Avis pointed to Figg. "But thanks for asking. That was kind of a thrill." She was a pretty woman, and the flush in her cheeks didn't make her any less so.

Mac waved away her response. "You need not feel so honored. Damon Devlin would find a way to check out the alibi of anyone who might have known the victim."

"But I didn't know him."

"You never met him?"

"No."

"Not even briefly at an author signing somewhere?"

"I didn't read his books. But wait! Mr. Figg did introduce me to him last night at the reception. I forgot about that." A suspicious person (me, for instance) might have suspected that she added that in case anyone had seen the two of them talking.

Mac nodded. "I see. And your sister, the other Tiffin"—he turned to her—"did you know Carter?"

"Bella Tiffin Grice." She pointed to her nametag to prove it. "I couldn't pick him out of a lineup. Are you going to ask me where I was when he was killed?"

"Damon Devlin would."

"Is he nuts?" the blond-haired man at Grice's side asked. He was looking at me, and tall enough to do it eyeball-to-eyeball.

"Sebastian McCabe is the sanest man in the world," I said. *Just don't ask me which world.*

"I was with my hubby in our room for two hours right after the book signing." Bella Tiffin Grice hugged him like Fitch hugged his bourbon. "Right, Larry?"

He turned pink. "Uh, right." *You crazy kids.*

Lynda looked at me and shrugged, as if to say *Well, that's that.* I thought I knew what she was thinking. A conspiracy of two in a romance-inspired murder was unlikely; a conspiracy of three, and one of them a husband, stretched credulity to the breaking point.

"This is daft," the British voice of Giles Hawthorne protested. "That was down time, the period before the Guest of Honor Event. Most of us were calling home, or checking social media, or using the toilet, or all of the above, and don't have anybody to verify it."

"I have pictures to show what I was doing then," Marcus Garber announced. "I was taking selfies for Facebook for half an hour. You can find them on my timeline."

"Excellent!" Mac said. "Still, you had a valid point, Mr. Hawthorne. Perhaps in this case Damon Devlin would have proceeded along different lines. You knew Rex Carter well, did you not?"

Hawthorne ran a hand through his salt-and-pepper hair, getting it out of his eyes. "I'm sorry he's dead, but I'm still right pissed at him." Melanie Swann, among others, let out a little gasp at this indecorous candor. "He blamed me for that turkey, *A Dragon for St. George*. It was his bloody plot, not mine. I just put words to it—about 90,000 of them, and as workman-like a job as I ever did—because he was having writer's block, like some rank amateur. And he got the byline and most of the money for minimal work. I was hard up at the time and jumped at the only deal that came my way. What did he have to complain about? I don't believe in that 'speak no ill of the dead' rot." *You sure don't.* "I may be a ghostwriter, but I'm not going to be silent." *Nice line, Giles. Save that for a book.*

"*De mortuis nihil nisi bonum* is perhaps an outmoded concept," Mac conceded. "You have plotted dozens of your own novels under various names, Mr. Hawthorne, so perhaps you would have done better. If this were a novel, and you were writing it, whom would you make the killer?"

It was about this point that I realized nobody else in the room was talking, not even in the corners. All ears were on Mac's sideshow.

"Somebody unexpected, of course."

"Of course. But whom?"

"What's the difference *whom* I would make the killer if this were a mystery novel, which it isn't?"

"Let us say that as a writer of mysteries myself, I am always curious about the creative process of my peers."

"Right. Well, then, how about Ned Seton? He's a bit an arse. Everybody here knows that he and Carter hated each other like poison, and I've heard rumors why. So from that point of view it would be plausible. But at the same time it would be a surprise. Who would expect an old man in a wheelchair to kill somebody for what you might call romantic reasons?"

"He isn't always in a wheelchair, to be strictly accurate," Lynda said. "When Jeff talked to him this evening he hobbled to the door on a cane."

"Hobbled is a good word for it," I confirmed, as much to remind Lynda as to inform everybody else. "I can't see him running around the hotel with his stick."

"So never mind that," Lynda said, "even though I love the idea of the unknown weapon being a sword-cane, like St. George sometimes carried. The irony would be delicious." *Yeah, to die for.* "But I still think Seton could have hidden the murder weapon in his wheelchair. The fact that he looked so helpless would have enabled him to get close enough to Rex Carter for a surprise attack."

Siegfried Van Cleef raised a glass of what looked like champagne, or maybe Sprite. Probably champagne. "I salute your ingenuity, young lady. What was this murder weapon that was so easily concealed?"

"We don't know."

"Judging by the hole in Carter's temple," I said, "it was probably something sharp, not exactly round, maybe a quarter-inch in diameter or a little more."

"Not a weapon per se, then," Van Cleef mused. "That takes us into Rex Stout territory. I've written about how often the Nero Wolfe stories involve unusual murder weapons. That is true from the beginning to the end of the corpus."

"The beginning being the golf club with the poisoned dart in *Fer-de-Lance*," said Mac, "and the end being the bomb in the cigar forty years later in *A Family Affair*." What a show-off!

"And between," Van Cleef riposted, "there were such delights as the pitchfork designed to look like goring by a bull in *Some Buried Caesar*, death by fumigation in *Door to Death*, the poisoned dart fired from a camera in *Easter Parade*."

Mac nodded. "And I have always been especially fond of *Black Orchids*, wherein Archie Goodwin is technically the murderer. He picks up a walking stick with a string attached and unwittingly pulls the trigger on a rifle, shooting a man to death in public."

"The victim is crushed by a statue of Benjamin Franklin in *The Final Deduction*," offered Melanie Swann, getting into the spirit.

Marcus Garber, with bride at his side, jumped in. "Those were all one-offs. There are at least three Nero Wolfe cases of murder by strangling—a telephone operator with her own cord, a dog owner with his own leash, and a cowboy with his own lasso."[8]

"You have an impressive command of some of the lesser-known works in the Wolfe corpus, Mr. Garber," Van Cleef observed.

"Well, I'm a big fan. Pierre LeGrande would like to be Wolfe's chef, Fritz Brenner, when he grows up."

Van Cleef nodded his large head with ostentatious slowness. "I see. I suppose that's why your LeGrande books themselves employ some unusual murder methods. As I recall, there was one where a rival chef was smothered in whipped cream."

"That's right. That was *Cream of the Crime*—my first book and still my favorite."

"And then there was the food critic crushed in a wine press—"

"*Vin de Mort*."

"—and the bomb in the wedding cake."

"*Bride and Boom*. That you remember my plots so well is flattering, although your reviews never have been."

---

[8] In *The Next Witness*, *Die Like a Dog*, and *The Rodeo Murder*, respectively, all novellas.

The critic shuddered theatrically. "One could hardly forget such, hmm, ingenuity."

Lisa Ballantine put a restraining hand on her husband's shoulder as if to hold him back. That wasn't the worst idea of the night. Garber looked like he had a short fuse, which had just been lit.

He took a deep breath before retorting: "Well, maybe I'll do something boring next time, like have the killer use a gun. I hold a concealed carry permit myself. Do you want to see my gun?"

He reached behind him. For a fleeting instant I had a mental picture of a crazed Marcus Garber engaging in a shootout with Mac, who practices with his Colt regularly. Sometimes I'd like to send my imagination on vacation.

"Marcus! Don't!" his wife snapped. "You know I hate guns."

And she wrote police procedurals! Go figure.

Garber brought his hand back, empty. "Okay, babe."

"This isn't fun anymore," Avis Tiffin announced.

"I don't think so either," Garber said, looking like he meant it. "Just for the record, I didn't know Rex Carter and I don't think I know anybody who did. Oh, and if you want to play another round of the alibi game, I was with Lisa all afternoon. We're on our honeymoon, after all."

Chapter Twenty-One
A Novel Idea

"Spouses are certainly convenient," Lynda said later, as we sat up in bed with our digital devices.

"I'll say." I moved closer.

"No, I mean as alibis. I was thinking of Bella Tiffin Grice and Marcus Garber. Convenient how they should both have been with their respective spouses at the critical time."

"That's not so surprising. I was with you."

"Hmm. Well, I'm still suspicious of Seton anyway. You don't write books like that without having a killer inside you somewhere." *I write books like that, Lyn. Or I used to. And maybe I will again!* "I'd love to be able to check out his wheelchair for a skewer or something."

"Fat chance. That's a job for the cops. Do you want to tell Captain Kritzer your idea?"

She shuddered prettily. "No thanks. And Mac is obviously not going to do it. I think their schoolyard fight is just so cute."

"That's not the word I would have used."

We went back to our devices. Cal Daley, Ed Decker's boss at Campus Security, had sent me a text with a link to the *Erin Observer & News-Ledger* story by Maggie Barton about Lani Alvarez. The old girl had spelled my name right and used all my talking points, so I had no complaints. Even better, she had quoted Lani's anticapitalist rant at length, which would cause most readers to write her off as a lunatic.

"Did you know that Klaus Bonhaus has been married five times and used to date our friend Heather O'Toole?" Lynda asked, looking up from her laptop.

Ms. O'Toole, familiarly known as H'OT in the tabloid headlines where the actress made frequent appearances, was actually more of an acquaintance than a real friend. We didn't exactly go to dinner at each other's houses. But she did give Lynda a beautiful dragonfly necklace as a gift after a spot of bother involving the vanishing of her uber-rich husband.[9]

"What are you doing, Lyn?"

"Reading up on The Tin Man. Looking at all the cute pictures of Donata that Mrs. McCabe posted on Facebook made me miss her too much, so I decided to give that a rest. The same with all the political rants on social media. So I've been doing a deep dive on Herr Bonhaus."

"Habsburg-Bonhaus."

"Yeah, him. Know thy enemy, I figure. I know enough now to be sure that if he takes over Grier, my job is toast."

I tossed my phone on the bed. "This is nuts. I'm working and you're worried about not working. We're supposed to be having a relaxing weekend." *Never mind the murder.*

"I'm worried about Johanna."

Lynda had guided the young reporter's career at the *Observer* ever since hiring her, and Tall Rawls still looked to Lynda as a role model.

"Johanna is young," I pointed out. "Isn't that what most news organizations are looking for these days—youth and inexperience that comes cheap? Frankly, she should

---

[9] See *The Disappearance of Mr. James Phillimore* (MX Publishing, 2013).

probably be moving on to a bigger paper anyway. She's certainly good enough."

"I thought maybe she should move into TV at one of the Grier stations, given the state of newspapers today."

"She'll do fine whatever her future holds. Talent will out." I sounded so confident I almost convinced myself. The truth is, a lot of talent is looking for work every day of the week.

"Well, then, what about me? What will I do if Bonhaus buys Grier and I don't make the cut when he starts gutting the staff?"

"You could be a stay-at-home mom. I've already told you we can afford it if that's what you want to do."

She got a dreamy look in her eye. "Actually, I think I'd love that. But I'd like to do something else, too—maybe more volunteer work at House of Serenity."

And then I said it. Don't ask me why. But Lynda says it was the inspiration of the Holy Spirit, and who am I to argue.

"You could write a book."

"What kind of book, *tesoro mio*?"

It's hard to concentrate when she opens wide those gold-flecked brown eyes and calls me her treasure, but I pressed on.

"Write what you like to read."

"I like mysteries, but I don't think I could plot one."

"I'm not so sure about that. Your solutions to the Carter murder were worthy of Ellery Queen himself." I haven't actually read much EQ, but that sounded good.

"That's different. I had a starting point." She shook her head, giving her soft honey-blond curls a minor workout. "No, I don't think I could write a mystery."

"Okay, then. The classic writing advice is 'write what you know.' So, write what you know."

"You mean journalism?"

"Or bourbon," I said with a chuckle. "Or bourbon and journalism together—that should be easy."

"You mean one of those big books, like a family saga?"

"Sure, why not?" *What's a family saga?* "And maybe a mystery would work into it somewhere. You have to have some suspense in any kind of book, whether it's murder, or backstabbing, or financial shenanigans at the family firm, or the romantic hanky-panky." *Hey, I'm on a roll. This sounds pretty good.* "In fact, you should start on that book whether you lose your job or not."

Lynda sat back against her pillows with a thoughtful look on her face. "You may be on to something there."

"You're welcome."

I leaned over. We kissed, etc.

Later, I picked up *The End of the Line*, the Melanie Swann paperback, and opened it for the first time.

CHAPTER I
Undercover Agent

"Anarchists, Chief?"

The little Scotsman shook his head. "I don't think so, Edwards. This may be merely criminal, not political. Our information is that these conspirators, whoever they are, plan to ask for ransom."

"I see."

For only the second time in his career, Birdy Edwards of the Pinkerton National Detective Agency was being briefed by Allan Pinkerton himself in his Chicago office. Whatever was up, it was big.

"I need you to go undercover. You're going to take a job on the railroad."

"And horses!" Lynda said.

I put down the book. "What?"

"If my novel's going to be about bourbon, it has to be set in Kentucky. So it should be about horses, too, and the Bluegrass region. I'll have to take some trips for research—Lexington, Georgetown, that area."

"Trips to distilleries?"

"Good idea!"

This is what passes for pillow talk in the Cody household.

I looked down at the book I was reading, with the author's name in bold letters at the bottom of the cover.

"Melanie Swann was right," I said. "A killer targeting mystery writers is just too corny."

"Maybe so, but this hotel would certainly be the place to do it right now."

Chapter Twenty-Two
A Widow's Regrets

The murder weapon is the key.

That's what I thought when I woke up on Sunday morning. It may have been the fragment of a forgotten dream, or it may have been the fruit of my subconscious plugging away at the problem all night, but the words were in my head when my eyes popped open.

And more than that, I had a nagging feeling that I had seen the weapon and not recognized it. But maybe that, too, was a remnant of dreamland.

To my surprise, Lynda lay at my side typing on her laptop. That, at least, was no dream.

"What are you doing?"

"I'm going to call it *Bluegrass*."

"You're going to call what *Bluegrass*?"

"My Kentucky family saga, of course! Wake up, sleepyhead. I've been working on plot ideas since about five o'clock. It's about the Breckenridge family, starting in the 1800s with two brothers. One goes into the horse business and the other one goes into the bourbon business. The book follows the descendants of both—two storylines which occasionally merge."

She filled in a surprising number of details. I didn't have to pretend to be impressed.

"You got that far in two hours? I think you're going to nail this fiction thing."

Smiling at the compliment, she resumed typing. Meanwhile, I caught up on the early media accounts of **MYSTERY WRITER KILLED AT MYSTERY CON,** as the *Cincinnati Sentinel* headlined it. The 99 cents I paid for a one-day subscription to the website so I could read the story wasn't a bad investment. Ziebart had done a creditable job, accurately quoting both Mac and me. Mac's "I am quite sure that Captain Kritzer has the case well in hand" came across as sincere in print, and I thought might even win him brownie points from his old nemesis. I could dream.

"Z's a good guy to have on the cop beat," Lynda observed from over my shoulder. "I wish he were part of the Grier team."

But neither Ziebart, nor Kindle, nor TV3 Action News told me anything I didn't already know about the murder, although the online reporter's account benefited from his on-the-scene perspective.

I did learn something, though: The girl with the dragon tattoo, Barbara Brant (a married name?), was good at her job. For surely she must have crafted the statement issued under Brent Harrison's name and quoted by all the news outlets, print and broadcast, at least in part:

"All of us at the Fountain Square Hotel are shocked and saddened by the death of the distinguished mystery writer Rex Carter. We extend our sincerest sympathy to his family, friends, and fans." *Expression of sorrow and sympathy, check.* "Our staff has been fully cooperating with law enforcement authorities as they seek to find his killer." *Assurance that we're not hiding anything, check.* "At the same time, we are reviewing all of our already-stringent security procedures to assure the safety of our guests, which is our highest priority." *There's no problem but we're fixing it anyway, check.*

With all that journalism under my belt after about fifteen minutes of reading, I went back to Melanie Swann's *The End of the Line* for a half-hour or so before getting ready for church. I paused from that pursuit now and then in a fruitless effort to recall something I had seen that could have been the murder weapon. It didn't necessarily have to be sharp, but it had to be hard.

Honesty compels me to admit that my concentration also flagged during 8:30 Mass with Mac and Kate at the Cathedral of St. Peter in Chains a few blocks from our hotel. I'd never been inside the beautiful Greek Revival church, which was built before the Civil War. But it wasn't the Corinthian columns and bronze doors that distracted me. It was thoughts of the murder. I also slipped in a few prayers for Rex Carter at the appropriate places.

"Excellent choir," Mac commented at the end of Mass, as we prepared to leave. "One feels that perhaps we just heard a foretaste of the heavenly chorus."

This was so obviously true that for once I had no sarcastic rejoinder, not even in my head.

As we walked down the aisle toward the big bronze doors at the entrance to the cathedral, I spotted a few familiar faces from QueenCon. Some I didn't know by name, but I identified Augustus Fitch and Aristotle O'Doul.

"There's Alison LeSourde," Lynda whispered.

She sat in a back pew, hands folded in her lap, apparently deep in prayer or thought.

"We must extend our condolences," Mac said.

Within a few minutes the cathedral had emptied out except for maybe a dozen or so worshipers, LeSourde among them. We walked over to her, Mac in the lead.

"Ms. LeSourde?"

She regarded us with her watery eyes. "Yes?"

"I am sorry to interrupt," Mac continued, "but we wish to extend our sympathy on your tragic loss."

"Oh. Thank you. You're Sebastian McCabe, aren't you?"

"I am. And these are members of my family." He introduced us. "Please be assured of our prayers."

"I need them." She stood up. "I'm not a very good Catholic."

"None of us is," Mac said.

She gave a half-smile. "I suppose that's true. If I were a better Catholic, I never would have married Rex—or Ned either, for that matter. But I'm trying to be a better one. My spiritual advisor assures me that it's never too late, like the last worker in the vineyard in the Gospel story. I find it helpful to go to Mass whenever I can, but especially on Sundays. Did you know that Andy Warhol attended Mass every day?"

"I did," Kate replied. *Well, sure.* "He was a Ruthenian Rite Catholic. I've used some of his paintings as examples of modern icons in my art classes. Like all Eastern Catholics, he was immersed in the presence of icons at his parish in Pittsburgh when he was growing up."

This artist-speak made my ears glaze over as we walked out of the cathedral into a bright April morning full of promise. Urban plantings still glistened with rain from the day and night before, but the forecast called for sunny and seventy. We all headed back to the hotel together. My ears only perked up again when LeSourde said:

"Who do you think killed Rex, Mr. McCabe? I know you've helped the police solve murders in your hometown."

Mac sighed. "I am afraid the situation is much different here. Admittedly, my in-laws and I have asked a few questions of people who knew your husband, and perhaps even formed a few tentative conclusions. However, Captain Kritzer of the Cincinnati Police Department has made it clear that he will brook no interference from me. We have a certain unfortunate history, the Captain and I, which complicates the situation."

"Kritzer? You mean the head honcho of Homicide? I was so stunned by this whole experience that I missed his name. He called me from Rex's cell phone. I was so relieved to get the call from that number. I thought it was Rex until he gave his name, followed by the word 'homicide.' Then I knew that something terrible had happened. I felt light-headed and I almost fainted."

"I bet he gave you the third degree," Lynda said.

"Is there such a thing as a fourth degree?" LeSourde stopped and pulled out a cigarette. Mac, an unreformed cigar smoker, lit it for her. "He obviously regards me as a suspect." *Suspect Number One, I'd say.* "But that's absurd! Why would I kill Rex? Quite apart from the fact that he was dying, we were happier together than we'd ever been. Since he stopped drinking, he'd abandoned a certain other bad habit as well."

"You mean he beat you when he was drunk?" Kate asked, concern etched in her fair face.

LeSourde looked shocked at the notion. "Lord, no, not that. His weakness lay in another direction. He used to go on book tours without me and sort of forget that he was married. Tours are almost a thing of the past now that there are so few bookstores around, but they used to be a bigger deal for fairly successful writers. Rex took full advantage of the women enthralled by the creator of Ian St. George. I knew that because I was one of them. Whatever made me think he would change after we got married? Old habits are hard to break, and that was a very old habit of Rex's. Still, I could comfort myself that he always came home in the end. And then eventually I stopped finding those little indications that he'd had female company while he was away. Not long after, a little over a year ago, he got diagnosed with the cancer. That was his reward for being a good boy. God's little joke. I don't know why I'm telling you all this. I guess I just had to tell somebody."

She thoughtfully blew smoke away from us.

"We will hold all of that in complete confidence, I assure you," Mac said.

"Did you tell Kritzer?" I asked.

"You mean about Rex's womanizing? He didn't ask, in so many words. He did want to know if my husband and I got along and I told him that we were very happy together. And that's the truth."

"That being the case, you will probably inherit everything under his will."

"Yes, of course. Our wills were identical, each making the other sole inheritor. Neither of us had any children, either together or separately—another regret of mine. At least, I don't *think* Rex had any children." She delivered her last line with more bite than habanero sauce.

"I am afraid that, in the limited imagination of Ricky Kritzer, that gives you a motive *par excellence*," Mac said.

"But Rex was dying!"

"He could have been planning to change the will," I pointed out, "and his untimely death would have stopped that."

"But he didn't have any such plans! Not that I know of, anyway. Why would he?"

Do you want a list of possible reasons?

By this time, we were standing outside the Fountain Square Hotel, enjoying a pleasantly cool breeze as ten o'clock approached. Lynda wrapped her gold and red pashmina tighter around her.

"What about Ned Seton?" she asked. "Wouldn't he have had a good reason to kill your second husband?"

"After all this time? Don't be silly. Besides, Ned may talk like a tough guy, but he's all bark."

"So you weren't afraid of those two being together at this conference?"

"No. That was never a concern." She tossed away her second cigarette since leaving Mass. "I was afraid of how I'd react. I hadn't seen Ned since I left him."

"And?" Lynda prodded.

"It was very awkward. I'd treated him so badly all those years ago that I had trouble looking at him. So I went to his room last night and apologized. It was hard work, and Ned didn't make it easy for me, but I got it done."

"If the killer's motive wasn't personal," Kate said, "it might have had something to do with your husband's writing, given that this hotel is host to almost two hundred mystery writers and fans right now."

The widow looked thoughtful. "I've heard of fiction writers getting threatening letters because of something they wrote, but if that ever happened to Rex he never told me."

"That reminds me," Mac said. "As the sole inheritor, you are in charge of the Rex Carter literary estate. It would be up to you to authorize other writers to carry on the St. George saga. Have you had time to consider—"

LeSourde shook her head. "That's not going to happen. Rex was very firm about that, and I promised to honor his wishes. Harry Fingerman already knows that. He probably thinks I'll change my mind and allow another writer to continue the series, but I won't. There isn't enough money in the world to make me go back on my word to Rex."

She spoke with a strength and determination that belied her willowy appearance.

"Ian St. George will go out just the way Rex wanted in *Murder, By George*," she added.

"How is it that Rex was able to overcome the writer's block that made it necessary for him to call in a ghostwriter for the previous St. George novel?" Mac inquired. "I ask only out of authorial curiosity."

"I think he was motivated by the unanimously bad reviews for *A Dragon for St. George*. I don't know how Rex ever let Harry talk him into using that hack Giles Hawthorne to write it. He couldn't write a grocery list.

"Once Rex got the idea for *Murder, By George*, he wrote like a demon, afraid that he wouldn't finish it. But, to tell you the truth, it's not that much better that Hawthorne's tripe. The plot creaks and the writing reads like a bad pastiche. Maybe it will sell well because it's the last St. George or because of Rex's murder. Harry thinks so."

"I loved your husband's books, Ms. LeSourde," Lynda said.

"Thanks. You're very kind. Many people did, but not so much over the last twenty years. He peaked as a writer before I met him. Harry doesn't seem to get that. The best of the St. George books were the ones he wrote in the 1980s. I think people still read them now for the nostalgia. The world was so different then. After all, that was a different millennium."

So who killed the has-been?

Suddenly I had a flashback to Winston's the night before. "Lynda and I came across Fingerman having before-dinner drinks with Aristotle O'Doul, one of America's greatest defense attorneys. Maybe he had good reason to prepare a defense."

"Alexian Rowe also was there," Lynda pointed out. "You don't think he was involved, too, do you?"

"Maybe Rowe just sat down with the other two. Or maybe it was conspiracy. Rowe said he's bought and sold first editions of the St. George books. Wouldn't they be worth more with the author dead?"

Lynda rolled her eyes.

"Okay, that's weak," I admitted.

"Rex and Harry went back a long way," LeSourde said.

"Familiarity breeds contempt," I quipped.

"Mr. Fingerman, as his agent, could have cheated your husband out of money and killed to cover up his crime, I suppose," Mac mused. "The money motive is never to be dismissed lightly."

LeSourde shook her head. "Harry may not be the world's smartest or most successful literary agent, but I don't believe there's a larcenous bone in his body."

Don't be too sure. You probably don't know all the bones in his body. Or do you?

We paused in the hotel lobby, as if reluctant to leave each other's company even though the first panel of the morning was fast approaching.

"I gather that your husband had no love lost for Hawthorne," Kate said to LeSourde.

"You could say that."

"So maybe the feeling was mutual."

"Hawthorne made his disdain for Rex clear rather publicly yesterday during a panel discussion and then again in Lafcadio Figg's hospitality suite last night," Mac observed.

"That's right!" Kate said. "I heard him at the party. We all did. He sounded like he hated Carter—maybe enough to kill him in a fit of anger. And if he did, maybe your life is in danger, too, Alison. You've been pretty vocal about Hawthorne to us, and I bet that wasn't the first time you've spoken out. If he's lost some potential work because of the things you and your husband have said about him, well, people have gone round the bend for less."

LeSourde looked like she wanted to believe, but couldn't quite make it. "Giles Hawthorne wouldn't have the nerve or the imagination to kill anybody!"

"Okay," Lynda said, "but what about Ned Seton? I know you think he's over you, but what if he isn't? You could be his next target."

The writer's widow looked from my wife to my sister, a strange expression on her face. "You ladies are scaring me. This is bizarre. I feel like I've fallen down the rabbit hole."

Lynda sent Kate a mental-telepathy message. At least, that's the way I read their eyeball exchange.

"Today's the last half-day of QueenCon," my sister said to LeSourde. "What are your plans?"

"Our hotel room is booked through the night and Captain Kritzer asked me to stay around. So I'm here for the rest of the day. But I'm certainly not going to any panels."

"I'm not either," Kate said. "Do you want some company?"

"I'd rather—" LeSourde stopped. "No, actually I'd like that. Thank you."

In reality, if the two most important women in my life (next to you, Mom) had some vague idea of protecting Alison LeSourde, Lynda would have been the better choice to stick with her. As one killer can already attest,[10] Mrs. (Teal) Cody is no slouch at taekwondo.

"And as for you, Sebastian," my sister added, "you've got to solve this thing! It's obvious that Kritzer isn't going to do it."

---

[10] See *The* 1895 *Murder* (MX Publishing, 2012).

Chapter Twenty-Three
Spiked?

Mac, Lynda, and I left the two women in the lobby and took the elevator up to the fourth floor for the final panels. Mac and Lynda slipped into "Holmes Away from Home: How Far Can New Interpretations Go?" while I checked out "Plot vs. Character" next door.

After two cozy writers, a past president of the Private Eye Writers of America, and the author of a police procedural series about a transgender Native American state trooper all agreed that character trumps plot, my panel broke up early. So I joined Mac and Lynda, taking an open seat near the back of the room. There were only two deerstalkers in the room, belonging to the matched male-female set that I'd noticed earlier at the opening reception. The male half of the duo, named Motherwell, had approached Mac for his autograph after Saturday's luncheon.

". . . hated the Baker Street Irregulars," Alexian Rowe was saying as I entered.

It turned out that he was talking about the brothers Conan Doyle, the two sons of Sir Arthur who outlived him. Apparently they managed their father's literary estate in a manner designed to squeeze every last farthing out of Sherlock Holmes in order to fund their wastrel ways. But that was ancient history. All the direct descendants of Arthur Conan Doyle were long gone, although a litigious estate remained. In recent years a court had ruled that

Sherlock Holmes, Dr. Watson, and associated characters were in the public domain, except those who appear only in a dozen stories still under copyright in the United States. I already knew about the legal gymnastics from Mac, and Ned Seton had alluded to the business during the conversation in his room.

"I can't imagine what Adrian and Denis would have thought of Benedict Cumberbatch as Holmes, much less Lucy Liu as Watson," said Phaedra Silchester, a middle-aged woman with Dracula-pale skin and bright red lipstick. Wasn't that kind of like mixing metaphors—or should I say "manifestations"? I learned later that Ms. Silchester wrote a popular series of steampunk graphic novels.

After the panel ended, I made a beeline for the tables set up in the hallway with coffee, Danish rolls, chocolate-filled croissants, fruit, bagels, cream donuts, and some of those healthful-seeming bran muffins laced with more fat and calories than plain donuts. It was quite a spread. Hungry from having skipped breakfast before Mass, I grabbed an 80-calorie container of yogurt. As I turned away so I wouldn't have to see Lynda's artery-clogging breakfast of choice, I almost ran into Olympia Fail.

"Oh, hi!" She licked chocolate off of her fingers. "So you're a Sherlockian, too!"

The Southern accent in which she delivered this comment is beyond my capacity to transliterate without making her seem like a bad actress in a low-budget movie. So just imagine it.

"No, I just hang around with people who are Sherlockians. But what made you say that?"

"I saw you at the last panel. Wasn't it fascinating?"

"Downright riveting," I lied.

"I liked it," Lynda stuck in, as if to argue. *What did I say?* She had a bagel in her hand, slathered with strawberry cream cheese. I had a feeling she would be hitting the gym hard next week.

"And it made me think," Fail went on, "wouldn't it be cool if somebody did a new twist on St. George—like make him a woman. Hey, maybe I should try that!"

You already have the eyepatch. After a moment's confusion, I realized that she was probably talking about trying her hand at writing an estrogen-endowed version of her hero as opposed to living it.

"You mean as fan fiction, just for fun?" Lynda asked.

"Of course!"

"I'd love to read it."

"What's your favorite St. George?"

"I think it's *All Cats Are Grey*, the one where—"

I slipped away. Resisting with great effort the siren song of a chocolate-filled pastry—I'm only human!—I found myself at a nearby table sadly littered with the remnants of what had once been numerous large piles of promotional gimmicks. I scanned it to see if I'd missed anything worthwhile the day before.

Standing next to Augustus Fitch, whom I studiously ignored, I picked up a four-inch metal replica of a railroad spike that I'd seen in my first go-round but paid little attention to. The tag attached said "Will this case be *The End of the Line* for Birdy Edwards?" on one side and had an image of the book cover on the other side.

I studied the spike. It had some weight and the end of it was pointed.

"How would you like to have that shoved in your temple?" came a whisper in my ear. Lynda stood next to me, a cup of coffee in her hand.

"I was just thinking the same thing. The shape looks about right."

"So maybe it wasn't Seton. Maybe it was Melanie Swann!" She kept her voice low. "Think of the irony—using a promotional item for her own book as a murder weapon.

No wonder she pooh-poohed the idea that somebody was out to kill mystery writers. She knew better."

I tried to let her down easy. "There were dozens of these sitting around yesterday. Anybody could have picked one up and jammed it into Carter. In fact, Swann would be about the last person likely to use one of these little beauties as a tool for murder. It would be like signing her name. Besides, what makes you think she'd want to kill Carter?"

"Why not? We've come up with motives for everybody else. What do we know about her?"

I tried to remember what she'd said about herself during the panel discussion. "She's written five books and Birdy Edwards is like the father she never knew. Also, she reminds me of Velma on *Scooby-Doo*."

Lynda rolled her eyes. "Very helpful." She pulled the program booklet out of her purse and opened it to the page with the author bios. "She lives in St. Louis, loves history, and has three cats."

"That looks deadly, Jefferson." Mac had arrived, a cream donut in his hand indicating that he had spent some time at the food table first. Before I even realized that he was talking about the little spike that I still had in my hand, Lynda said: "We were just discussing the possibility that it could have been *very* deadly."

Mac raised an eyebrow. "Indeed! It is not hard to imagine that having this in hand during a moment of anger could lead to deadly consequences. It might have even been self-defense, after which the killer panicked." He took the item out of my hand and studied it.

"Maybe we should tell Kritzer." Did I really say that? I'll never know how Mac would have responded, because at that moment Kate and Alison LeSourde joined the party.

"Kritzer called Alison on her cell phone again," Kate announced.

"That cannot be good," Mac muttered darkly.

Chapter Twenty-Four
Body Number Two

"He wants us to meet him in Board Room One," Kate said. "It's on the mezzanine. The hotel set it aside for him to do interviews."

"We shall accompany you," Mac said. He addressed LeSourde: "If the Captain appears less than happy to see me, pay no attention."

This is no time for jokes, Mac.

"You are really very kind and I am grateful for that," LeSourde said. "I just don't have the strength to do this by myself right now."

Aside from a slight throbbing of the vessels in his thick nick, Kritzer didn't allow himself to show any emotion at the committee of four that Alison LeSourde brought with her. He still had us outnumbered, although the lieutenant, the two sergeants, and the two investigators let the big guy do the talking.

"What is it that you couldn't tell me on the phone, Captain?" LeSourde asked.

"The kind of news we try not to convey that way, I'm afraid." He paused. "And let me point out that I didn't invite you to bring friends with you."

"Still, if you don't mind, I'd prefer that they stay. They aren't friends, exactly, but I think that they will be."

"We promise not to speak unless spoken to, Captain." Mac put just the slightest emphasis on his old nemesis's title.

"All right, then." *Nobody will accuse Dick Kritzer of acting like a . . . of being unreasonable.* He watched LeSourde carefully as he said, "Your former husband, Edward Seton, was found dead in his hotel room a short while ago by housekeeping. His head was split open."

The double-widow gasped and looked like she was going to faint. I've read of the blood draining from somebody's face, but this may have been the first time I ever actually saw it happen. My sister put her arms around LeSourde, as much to keep the woman from falling as to comfort her. Was LeSourde acting? Maybe, but I didn't think so.

"Somebody killed him?" she asked.

"That's what it looks like. But it's not a lock at this point. Somebody from the coroner's office should be here soon. Sometimes they can tell from a quick look at the body whether it's natural, or accident, or whatever. That's not our job. Right now, though, I'm proceeding on the assumption that this is another homicide investigation."

Barbara Brant, the marketing and crisis communications consultant, would have her hands full now. On the plus side for her, she'd be getting a lot of billable hours out of this homicide spree. She could use the money to replace the hair she would be pulling out.

Avis Tiffin's crazy idea in the hospitality suite last night about a mass murderer picking off mystery writers suddenly didn't seem so crazy.

"Was the wound in the temple?" Mac asked Kritzer, perhaps because serial killers tend to use the same modus operandi.

"Forehead. I gather that Mr. Seton was quite a bit older than you, Ms. LeSourde."

"Yes. I'm fifty-seven. I was young and foolish when I married him. Now I'm middle-aged and foolish."

"A witness tells us that you visited Seton late last night."

"Who, might I ask, was this witness?" Mac said.

"You can ask but I won't tell you." The expression on Kritzer's face strongly suggested that he'd been born to say that and that it was a very clever retort indeed.

Alison LeSourde sat down in the nearest available chair. "It wasn't that late—about eight o'clock, I think. Maybe a little earlier."

"He was alive when you left?"

"Of course he was!"

"As a matter of fact, he was—that time. But you could have come back. The witness heard Seton calling after you when you left, before the door was all the way closed. She couldn't hear the words but she said it didn't sound very nice."

LeSourde bit her lip. I know a woman craving a cigarette when I see one, having been in love with Lynda during her smoking days. "No, it wasn't very nice. The visit started out well but it went downhill when I made the mistake of reminding him that I was the only woman who ever left him. I don't know why I said that. It was stupid, stupid, stupid. Saying something like that was the furthest thing from my mind when I asked to meet with him. It's certainly not why I went there. But I'd forgotten how arrogant Ned could be, and his condescension annoyed me. He became beastly and said that people would think that I killed Rex."

"Why would he say that?"

"Because he knew it would hurt me."

"Not because it was true?"

She shook her head. "No, no, and he knew that."

"How would he know that, Ms. LeSourde?"

"Because he knew me. You referred to him as my former husband, so you know that we were once married."

"Yes. And, as I understand it, you left him for Mr. Carter."

This wasn't exactly the third degree, there not being a single bright light being shined in her eyes, but Alison LeSourde looked like she'd rather be anywhere else.

"That's right, seventeen years ago."

"That's a long time. Why did you go to his room last night if not to remind him that you were the only woman who ever left him?"

"To say that I was sorry."

"That you left him?"

She sighed. "Maybe it would have gone better if I'd left it at that. But the truth is, and this is what I told him, that I'm sorry for all of it—marrying him, falling in love with Rex, divorcing Ned, hurting him. But it all began with marrying him, so I had to start with that. Ned didn't appreciate my honesty. He had to know our marriage was wrong from the first, but he didn't like me being the one to say it. At least, that's the way I interpreted what happened. At any rate, I bungled it. I bungle everything."

"I'm sure that's not true!" Kate averred.

LeSourde shot her a grateful look. "Still, I'm glad I tried. I'm glad I got to see him one last time."

Seton had assured me that he felt no animosity toward Carter and LeSourde, and that he and his third wife were better off apart. But that had been shortly before her visit. He might have had a different take on the past with her in front of him in his hotel room. The proximity could have re-stoked some old passions, romantic or resentful or both. It wasn't hard to imagine the situation getting away from the former couple, with both of them saying things they would regret later—except that later never came for Seton.

Alison LeSourde put her hands in her lap, long fingers intertwined. I wondered if she was praying.

"I'm sorry to have to ask you these questions, Ms. LeSourde," Kritzer lied. Or maybe he really was sorry. But I doubted it. "What prompted you to reach out to Seton with this apology, if that's what it was, after all these years?"

"Desire met opportunity, Captain. He was here, which made it easy. And I wanted to do it because the ninth step—you know about the steps?"

"A little bit."

Don't take this to the bank, but I had a suspicion that Kritzer had more than a passing acquaintance with twelve-step programs.

"The ninth step is to make amends," LeSourde continued, perhaps unnecessarily. "I'm not really sure that's possible for me, given what I'd done to Ned. How do you unbreak an egg or unbreak a man's heart? But I at least wanted to say I was sorry. Rex's death made me realize that we are all on borrowed time, especially a man who is almost ninety-three years old. But I botched it. I screwed up royally."

Kate, standing behind her, put a comforting hand on her shoulder.

"You said you got to Mr. Seton's room around eight o'clock," Kritzer reminded her. "Our witness said you left around eight-thirty, so that checks. That still seems a little late to me."

"I was eating dinner outside the hotel when it came to me, what I had to do. I walked around a while to get up the nerve. Then I called his hotel room, but he didn't answer. I tried again about ten minutes later and that time he picked up. I asked if I could come and see him and he agreed."

"I can confirm that, Captain," I said. I'd heard the phone ring both times, the first while I was sitting with Seton and the second just after I'd left his room and the door closed shut. I explained that, earning an "okay" and a nod from Kritzer.

"What was he like when you left?" Kritzer asked LeSourde.

"Agitated, completely different from when I arrived. I'd managed to push just the wrong buttons on Ned."

"Where were you when he died?"

"When was that?"

Kritzer looked at his colleagues, but if they gave any indication of how they thought he should answer, I didn't detect it.

"It must have been sometime between nine and nine-thirty this morning," he said.

Mac raised an eyebrow at the tight timeframe.

"He ordered breakfast at nine o'clock," Kritzer said. "When room service was delivered a half an hour later, using a pass key to get in, he was dead. The server called nine-one-one immediately. Lt. DeVore and I were already in the hotel."

"We saw Ms. LeSourde at eight-thirty Mass at the Cathedral," Kate said. She hadn't promised Kritzer to keep quiet. "Mass wasn't over until nine-thirty or so."

Kritzer frowned. "Thank you, Mrs. McCabe. That's very helpful. Were you actually with her during the service?"

"Not sitting with her, no. But—"

"Since you asked," Mac told Kritzer, "I did happen to notice Ms. LeSourde when we entered church. I also saw her later, at the sign of peace and at communion." *Meanwhile, some of us were praying, not people-watching.* "Then, after Mass, we four spoke with her and walked with her back here."

"I know this must be a very difficult time for you, Ms. LeSourde," Kritzer told her. "You were obviously still in shock when we talked yesterday afternoon. In the time since, have you had any thoughts about who might have killed your husband—Rex Carter, I mean? Or even how?"

"No. No, I have no idea."

Like an idiot, I cleared my throat. "About the murder weapon, Captain, I did want to call something to your attention."

He looked at me as if I were a specimen. "You?"

I pulled the small replica railroad spike out of my pocket and handed it to him. He stared at it.

"What the hell is this?"

"It's a marketing ploy to advertise a book called *The End of the Line*. The author is here at QueenCon. There must have been three or four of these sitting out on a table of freebies yesterday, or maybe more. It looks to me like it could have made the hole that I saw in Carter's temple."

Kritzer's beefy hand closed around the spike. "Shape's about right. The diameter might be a little small, but it's hard to tell for sure. Anyway, we had a very different tip about the murder weapon that we're checking into right now."

"A sword cane?" Lynda asked hopefully.

"That's an ingenious idea, Ms. Teal." The tone of Kritzer's voice said otherwise. "But why would the killer stop there? Why not use an exploding cigar?"

"Rex Stout already did that," Mac offered. "In fact, he did it twice—early in his career and then at the very end."

For a few seconds I thought Kritzer would have an explosion of his own, but I give him major points for getting his blood pressure down in a hurry. Or maybe Mac was just lucky that one of the homicide detectives slipped into the room and shook his head at Kritzer.

The Captain sighed like an unhappy elephant. "You can go now, Ms. LeSourde, and the rest of you, too."

"Thank you. Does this mean—"

"You'll be happy to know that the surveillance video of the relevant portion of the eighth floor hallway shows you leaving your former husband's room last night and not returning this morning."

"Ah, then you have another suspect," Mac said.

Kritzer glared. "Nobody entered that room this morning."

Relief cut a few years off of LeSourde's apparent age, but my mind was elsewhere. "If they have a video surveillance system," I said, "shouldn't that show Carter's murder?"

"Only the floors with guest rooms are covered, Cody, but thank you for your help."

He didn't mean that, in case you were wondering.

The door had barely closed behind us when we saw the petite form of Lisa Ballantine coming up the stairs.

"Ha!" she cried. "You beat me to it."

"How so?" Mac asked mildly.

"The cops! Last night I left the hospitality suite and went to the second floor. The crime scene tape was up, but no cops were around. Very disappointing. But Melanie Swann just told me she saw a bunch of cops up here on the mezzanine."

So she didn't know about Ned Seton; she was just riding her hobby horse of police procedural research.

"Ms. Swann was correct," Mac said. "Captain Kritzer and his crew have set up in Board Room One to conduct interviews."

"Thanks."

"How's your husband?" Lynda asked.

"He's still sulking," Ballantine reported. "He'll get over it eventually. We really have to work on his temper."

She took off toward Board Room One without ever having acknowledged, or perhaps noticed, Alison LeSourde.

Chapter Twenty-Five
The Witness

"Just what Kritzer needs—a mystery writer under foot," I said.

"Precisely." Mac unwrapped a cigar. "He may regret his dismissal of me when he finds Ms. Ballantine even less palatable."

"Don't be so sure," Lynda said. "He may like her."

"You can't smoke that in the hotel." I pointed unnecessarily at the cigar.

"No, but I can use my imagination—a faculty with which the Captain is under-equipped. For example, how does he know that the person who called for room service under Seton's name was actually Seton? It could have been the killer, or the killer's accomplice, establishing a false time of death for alibi purposes."

"Do you believe that?" Kate asked.

"No, I only think that it is possible. Certainly whoever answered the phone would not be familiar with Edward Seton's voice, making the impersonation quite simple. No acting skills would be required."

"Yes, I can see that," said Alison LeSourde. "Thanks for not sharing the idea with Captain Kritzer."

"Giving Kritzer ideas is the last thing he wants to do," I informed her. "Not until he can serve up the killer on a plate with an apple stuffed in his mouth. Or hers."

Smiling, Mac stuck the unlit cigar in his mouth. *At least it wouldn't explode.* The cigar didn't stop him from talking. Nothing ever does. "Someone has certainly put you in the Captain's cross-hairs, Ms. LeSourde. I would like to know the identity of the convenient witness who made you a person of interest in Ned Seton's death as well as Rex Carter's."

"We don't even know that Seton was murdered," I reminded everybody. "The man was almost ninety-three and visibly in poor shape. What are the odds that *two* men on the fast track to their final resting places would be murdered by an impatient killer? I'd say not very high. Whether Seton was killed is a real question in my mind."

"Quite so," Mac rumbled. "And the question is not a minor one. If we are looking for a killer who had a reason to kill both Rex Carter and Edward Seton, then that complicates our task tremendously. There might be two motives or one. Who did the two victims, if there are two victims, have in common?"

"Me," LeSourde said. "There's no getting around that."

"Also Paul Malvern and Siegfried Van Cleef," I put in. "Both of those guys wrote about both of those guys." I knew what I meant.

"Precisely," Mac said again.

But LeSourde, displaying no self-serving instinct to boost a handy suspect, said: "Why would Paul want to kill Rex or Ned? Wouldn't it be more likely he'd find out something about one of them during his researches that they'd kill to hide?"

Not that again! Next she'll be saying what a dandy murder victim Van Cleef would make.

"And, of course, half the mystery writers in America would like to throttle that horrible Van Cleef."

See.

Mac cleared his throat. "I must confess that his reviews of my own humble works have not always been wholly complimentary." I suspected that Mac was indulging in understatement here, but I made a habit of not reading reviews of his unending stream of Damon Devlin escapades. Who has that kind of time? "Never mind that, however. What was your relationship with Paul Malvern, Ms. LeSourde?"

"Well, he interviewed me at great length several times. I suppose you could say I was an important resource for his biography of Rex."

"Only that?"

"We're friendly, but I don't really know—oh, I see what you mean! Some sort of *crime passionnel*. Don't be absurd! I'm old enough to be Paul's mother."

Old enough to be . . . Something about that phrase seemed familiar, but the memory—if that's what it was— was elusive as a butterfly.

"Surely you of all people know that age is merely a number," Mac pressed. "You married two men older than yourself, the first of whom easily could have been your father, biologically speaking."

"And it was a big mistake. I'm not playing games with you, Mr. McCabe. Paul Malvern had no interest in me other than as a source of information about his subject. Frankly, I found our conversations a duty rather than a pleasure."

"So there is no clear motive there. That leaves one other person who, as Jefferson noted, had a relationship with both of your husbands."

"Siegfried Van Cleef was nasty to both of them, in reviews in print and here at QueenCon, if that's what you mean by a relationship."

"When I talked to Seton last night, he offered Van Cleef as a suspect in Carter's murder," I said. "He didn't have anything very strong, just that maybe Van Cleef had done something to Carter, and Carter threatened to expose him for it."

LeSourde shook her head. "That doesn't sound right. First of all, I can assure you that Rex hasn't been threatening to expose anybody. He's been in no shape for it. Until recently, he was conserving all of his energy to finish the last St. George book. And since then, he's been resting up for this conference. Besides, I'm pretty sure that Rex didn't know any deep, dark secret about Van Cleef. The man's a nasty narcissist with delusions of style, but that's hardly a secret."

"Rex would have told you if he knew something damaging about Van Cleef?" Lynda asked.

"I think so. We talked a lot."

"I said the idea wasn't strong," I noted. "But Van Cleef had a good reason for killing Seton, if you think revenge is a reason. In addition to whatever money was involved in Van Cleef's settlement with Seton for copyright infringement, the old guy must have embarrassed him and hurt his reputation."

"But still," Lynda said, "that only covers a motive for killing Seton."

"Perhaps there are two murderers, with two different motives," Mac said.

LeSourde put her hand to her head. "I have a headache."

"How about some herbal tea?" Kate said. "I have some in our room."

"That sounds good."

They headed for the elevator. Watching them go, I found myself hoping that Kate's new BFF didn't turn out to be something other than the fragile, penitent, recovering woman that she seemed.

Sebastian McCabe contemplated his unlit cigar, while Lynda pulled out her smartphone.

"I think I'm catching Ms. LeSourde's headache," I said.

Mac ignored me. "Perhaps, since we are not even certain that Seton was murdered, it would be best to concentrate on method rather than motive—the method in the first and undisputed murder, I mean."

"That's what I woke up thinking this morning—that the method is the key!" I was proud of myself.

"Murder or not," Lynda said, looking up from her phone, "Seton's exit from this veil of tears is public knowledge now. It's on the QueenCon Facebook page. 'QueenCon XI extends our sympathy to Alison LeSourde, former spouse of Guest of Honor Edward "Ned" Seton, who unexpectedly passed this morning. A great talent whose Jason Darke stories have recently attracted a new generation of admirers, he will be missed.'"

"Avis has really been on the ball with social media this weekend," I said. "But I'm not so sure that particular post was a good idea. It might make the conference survivors nervous." *And by the way, it's a good thing they didn't stuff the swag bags with "I SURVIVED QUEENCON XI" T-shirts.*

Mac pulled out his own phone. "Ah, I see that Lafcadio has called me several times this morning."

He punched "Return Call" and activated the speakerphone function.

"Hello, Lafcadio, I suspect that you are calling me about the sad news of Edward Seton's death."

"It would have been news if you'd answered your phone," Figg groused in a non-too-pleasant tone of voice. "Everybody following the con on Facebook knows by now—I had Avis post it."

"And how did you know about it?"

"The hotel manager, Harrison, called me. He thought I'd want to know."

"Have you talked to Captain Kritzer about it?"

"No. Should I call him?"

"I thought perhaps he called you. Homicide is investigating."

Lafcadio Figg uncharacteristically responded with several few words of only one syllable each, none of which bear recording here.

"Most distressing," Mac agreed. "Still, it is quite possible that this latest death is natural after all."

Figg uttered more short words, and then, "If this mess doesn't get resolved, and soon, it may mean the end of QueenCon. Damn it, Sebastian, you've got to do something!"

A look of beatific satisfaction crossed Mac's face at this plea for help from his old antagonist (or *bête noir* in Mac-speak).

"We can but try, Lafcadio."

"Do you have any leads?"

"A witness reported seeing a certain person leave Edward Seton's room last night. That seems suspiciously convenient to me. I should like to know who that witness was, and Ricky Kritzer refuses to tell me." *Why would he, even if he wasn't carrying a grudge older than* The Simpsons? *He's a cop; you're a civilian.* "I should like very much to identify that witness and talk to her."

"Her?"

"Ricky distinctly said 'she.' Knowing that this observant citizen is a woman does narrow the field a bit."

"To every woman in the hotel, you mean?"

"Hardly that. The witness most likely has a room on the eighth floor, along the same corridor with the late Ned Seton. It would be no great task for us to call every woman on the floor. I presume you have the registration records?"

"Avis has them. She could e-mail you the spreadsheet, but it will probably be easier if I have her bring you a printed copy. Where are you now?"

"Tell her we will meet her on the fourth floor, where the panels are. She is probably there already."

"She is—right here with me." Figg gave the sigh to end all sighs. "What a disastrous weekend. Please keep me posted."

"You can be sure of that." *So I can gloat.* Mac disconnected.

"Mr. McCabe!"

"The press has arrived," I muttered to Lynda. It was Joe Ziebart, the police reporter for the *Cincinnati Sentinel* e-newspaper.

"My sources in the CPD tell me that Homicide is investigating another possible murder and that Kritzer and crew are camped out on this floor," Ziebart announced.

"Is that so?" Mac said.

"You mean you didn't know?"

"Did I say that?"

Mac fenced well for such a heavy guy.

"Well, do you have any thoughts about Edward Seton's death?"

The way the dialogue was going, I expected Mac to say something like, "Should I?" But instead of answering the question with another question, he said, "For most of his long career, Edward Seton was an underpaid and underappreciated exemplar of the hard-boiled school of detective fiction. I am pleased that in recent years his work has finally achieved proper critical attention."

"But about the possibility that he was murdered—"

"You will want to speak to Captain Kritzer. We just left him in that room." Mac pointed down the hall at Board Room One.

"He interviewed you? Or are you helping him with the case?"

"You will have to excuse me, Mr. Ziebart. We have an elevator to catch."

Lynda shrugged at the reporter. *Sorry, Z. Not my fault.* But as we hustled down the corridor, she went back to her smartphone. "Morrie will want to know about this," she muttered as she texted.

Most of the panels—the last ones of the conference—apparently had just let out before the elevator delivered us to the fourth floor to find Avis Tiffin. Conventioneers still milled about in the foyer, which looked rather naked without a breakfast bar or ice cream social. A few pieces of luggage were stacked here and there by conference participants who had checked out of their rooms. Alison LeSourde may not have been the only one staying the night, but that wasn't the common thing.

"QueenCon has certainly thinned out," Lynda observed. "This was much more crowded an hour ago."

"Some participants always leave early on the final day of a conference because of plane departure times, the need to get home, and so forth," Mac said. "I only hope that does not bode ill for our inquiries."

"Don't you think the killer would make it a point to stay to the bitter end, so as to not rouse suspicion?" I said.

"A mystery writer might think that way, yes. At any, rate, Lafcadio and Ms. Tiffin are here, as promised."

They stood at what had been the registration desk, littered with spreadsheets. Figg walked back and forth, apparently so nervous that he forgot to be pompous. He stopped pacing when he saw Mac.

"Sebastian!"

Mac nodded a greeting. "Ms. Tiffin, did Lafcadio tell you what we need?"

Far from being dressed in mourning clothes, Figg's ace volunteer was decked out in a bright orange and yellow blouse over white slacks. The outfit shouted spring.

"He said you wanted to know who was on the eighth floor of the hotel, especially anybody whose room was close to Mr. Seton."

"Precisely."

"I'm sorry. That's not in our records. If you remember, all QueenCon guests made their hotel reservations separately. So we don't have anybody's room number."

"I see. Well, I suppose I shall have to go to Mr. Harrison for that information."

"But I'm on the eighth floor, Mr. McCabe. Maybe I can help."

"Perhaps." He sounded skeptical. "The point of my query is to find the woman who told Captain Kritzer's men that she heard Mr. Seton engaged in a bit of an imbroglio with a woman leaving his room last night."

"Oh!" Her face made an exclamation point. "I guess that would be me."

Chapter Twenty-Six
The Vanishing of the Lady

That rated two raised eyebrows from Mac, which I believe translated to *"Occasionally one does get lucky."*

"I'm not sure what an imbroglio is," Tiffin continued, "but I heard him yell after her and slam the door. That's what I told the police."

"What exactly did he say?"

"He said, 'People will think you killed Rex. You know that, don't you? They will always think it, whether you get charged or not.'"

"And how did Ms. LeSourde respond?"

"Was that the woman he was yelling at?"

"Yes."

"Oh. I don't know her. She didn't say anything, but she was crying as she ran down the hallway. So much drama! Honestly, I didn't think anything of it until this morning when I heard a lot of commotion outside my door and it turned out to be the cops. Apparently room service or the manager or somebody had called them about the body. Even then, I wanted to just close the door and stay out of it, but Siegfried said we should tell what we heard."

"Siegfried?" Lynda repeated, taking the word right out of my mouth.

Avis Tiffin colored. "Mr. Van Cleef. He was, uh, with me."

"This morning?" Mac clarified.

"Yes. Well, all night."

Apparently not everybody hates Van Cleef, and he doesn't hate everybody. Who would have guessed?

Mac arched an eyebrow. "Indeed. In that case, I should like to speak to him."

"That won't be hard. He's right behind you."

We turned around. Van Cleef hovered, a look of impatience on his full face as he looked toward Tiffin. "Ready to leave, my dear?"

Was he taking her home or vice versa? Don't ask me. I go out of my way to not know that kind of thing.

"Ready when you are, Siegfried!" Tiffin said.

Maybe I shouldn't have been surprised that fifty-something Siegfried Van Cleef had found romance at QueenCon XI. After all, Marcus Garber and Lisa Ballantine married there. And Tiffin undoubtedly found the attentions of the best-known living mystery critic flattering, given her mystery-writing ambitions. But as for Van Cleef, I'd figured he was already in love with himself.

"Oh, hello, Siefried," Mac said. "We were just having a most interesting conversation."

The critic smirked. "I'm not surprised. Ms. Tiffin is a delightful conversationalist, as I have come to know over these last two days."

"She tells us that you insisted on informing the police about Edward Seton's contretemps with his former wife last night."

The critic hesitated, probably trying to figure out Mac's angle before answering. "Yes, that's right. I always try to do my civic duty."

"Most admirable. Was that the only reason?"

"What do you mean? What other reason could there be?"

"It is hard not to notice that this puts Ms. LeSourde in a very awkward position."

"Well, what of it? I can't help that, can I? I don't believe I've ever met the woman, not that it would matter."

Lynda's phone rang. She walked away from us as she said "hello."

"The police believe that Edward Seton died between ordering breakfast and its delivery," Mac continued. "Did you observe anything of interest this morning?"

"Playing detective, are you, McCabe? I don't have to play along, you know, but I see no harm in it. No, we saw nothing untoward. If I had, you can rest assured I would have reported it to the police."

"You did not, for example, observe Howard Fingerman or Paul Malvern leave room eight twenty-three? That would not have been untoward, as you put it, but it might have been significant."

"So those are the trees you're barking up? No, we didn't see them or anyone else. But then, I must admit that Ms. Tiffin and I were otherwise occupied this morning."

Stop right there. And wipe that smirk off your face!

"No doubt you two were also getting acquainted between the book signing yesterday and the discovery of Rex Carter's body?" Mac said amiably.

Van Cleef smiled, strongly reminding me of the Grinch, except with a fuller face. "That's quite true. Isn't it my dear?"

"Yes." She squeezed the word out as if grudgingly.

So Avis Tiffin and her indiscreet lover conveniently alibied each other, just as Arabella Tiffin Grice and Mr. Grice did. And the newlyweds, too! Maybe I should call this *The Case of the Mutual Alibis*.

Mac didn't appear especially disappointed, and I could understand why. Even Seton had admitted that his suggestion of Van Cleef as the murderer of Rex Carter had no basis beyond his knowledge of the man's character. The speculation that Carter had been a threat to the critic rested on sand, although Van Cleef clearly had reason to be annoyed at Seton.

"For the record," Van Cleef added, "the deaths of Carter and Seton were a double blow to me. I always found rich veins of material for commentary in their attempts at writing."

"Even Seton, who sued you?" I said.

My attempt to get a rise out of him an utter failure, he shrugged. "Occupational hazard. I made a mistake. I can hardly cavil about paying the price."

Avis Tiffin turned to Figg, who had been admirably silent for the past quarter-hour. "I don't feel so well all of a sudden. Is it okay if I go home now?"

"Yes, of course. We have enough volunteers for clean-up. Thanks for all your help. You've been invaluable."

She nodded, tossed a "nice to have met you" to Van Cleef over her shoulder, and sauntered out. After picking his metaphorical jaw off the metaphorical floor, her weekend wooer decided to go after her. "Avis!" he called on the fly. She kept walking, not even turning around. *You go, girl!*

Lynda came back from the huddle with her phone. "That was Morrie Kindle calling. He thought I'd like to know the coroner got a look at Seton's body."

"*The* coroner?" I said. Back home in Sussex County, much smaller than Cincinnati's Hamilton County, the coroner seldom showed up at prospective crime scenes in person. She had a small but competent core of crime scene people to handle that.

"Yeah. He likes to be called in on the big-publicity cases and he was irritated that he couldn't be reached at a party last night. That's according to Morrie's well-placed sources. So this morning his staff called him off the links. He took one look at the small amount of blood in the open wound and decided Seton must have had a stroke or heart attack in his wheelchair. The autopsy will tell which. He apparently died, then fell out of the chair and hit his head, probably on the edge of the minibar."

"So we're back where we started," I said, proving once again my keen perception of the obvious. "One murderer and one victim."

"Also one murder method," Mac noted.

"Since Seton wasn't murdered, that makes it more plausible that he killed Carter," Lynda reasoned. "There doesn't have to be two murderers, or one murderer with a reason to kill both. I still like the idea of a sword in his cane. Or maybe a stiletto."

"Stiletto?"

"Yeah, as in stiletto heel, without the heel."

I didn't think this analogous reference to women's fashion would mean anything to Sebastian McCabe, he not exactly being a fashionista. (He wears bow ties.) But I was wrong. He raised an eyebrow. "By thunder, I do believe you are on to something, Lynda!"

"On to what, exactly?"

"The murder weapon, of course."

"Join the crowd," I quipped. "I distinctly remember your pal Kritzer saying he had a lead on that."

"Police investigate many leads. Perhaps the one about the weapon will prove fruitful, but that is by no means certain. Meanwhile, I had best act quickly. QueenCon XI is history and people are leaving."

He looked around. The ranks had thinned even more while we'd been talking. A few conference-goers milled around—I spotted Fingerman talking to Augustus Fitch, for instance (striking a deal that would help Fitch to break out of self-publication?)—but in general the scene reeked of "see you next year." Conventions always limp to a close like that, in my experience, whether professional in nature or a confab of hobbyists.

"Let us try the lobby," Mac said, moving toward the elevator as he walked.

"Are you thinking that Seton really had a gimmicked cane?" Lynda asked.

"By no means, dear Lynda. Whatever gave you that idea?"

"You! You said I was on to the murder weapon!"

"Your comment gave me a notion that I need to verify. I only hope the person I want to see—ah, here we are!"

We were now in the lobby, where QueenCon stragglers said their goodbyes by exchanging hugs and, in some cases, business cards. Mac strode over to the familiar figures of Paul Malvern and Olympia Fail, who seemed to be together.

"What's the good word?" Malvern asked when he saw my brother-in-law heading his way. Even his ponytail looked dispirited.

"I am afraid that I have none. Have you been on social media recently?"

"No, I was on the last panel, 'What Makes a Great Mystery Writer.' Why?"

"If you had been, you would have learned that Edward Seton died this morning."

"You're kidding!"

Why do you always say that, Paul?

"What!" That came from Olympia Fail, her good eye wide. "I can't believe it! Heart attack or something like that? Or was it an accident?"

"There is a third alternative," Mac pointed out, "that of murder."

"Oh. I didn't think of that."

"Strange that you did not, Ms. Fail, given the precedent this weekend. However, it is our understanding that the coroner quickly determined from personal observation that Seton's death was due to natural causes."

As Mac spoke, he looked at Fail's feet, decked out in black flats, and then back up to her face. She wore a zebra-striped blouse over gray slacks. "Rex Carter, on the other hand, was definitely murdered. And I believe I know how."

Fail put her hand to her mouth. "Excuse me." She took off toward the ladies' room. *Tummy trouble?*

Mac's eyes never left her retreating form.

"Okay, what gives?" Lynda asked.

Before Mac could respond, Kritzer and the team from Homicide got off the elevator. Joe Ziebart and—believe it or not—Lisa Ballantine tagged close behind. The Captain carried in his hand a pair of red high heels that didn't match his outfit. I knew those shoes!

"The murder weapon, I presume," Mac said.

"Looks like it, judging by the dried blood on the bottom of the right one."

"Where and how did you find them?"

"They were in a trash can in a vending alcove on the sixth floor, just where our tipster said they would be."

"Ah, another helpful citizen! Who was it this time?"

"I wouldn't tell you if I knew. Some woman."

"I had a notion about these fatal shoes when Lynda used the word 'stiletto' in her fantasy about a weapon hidden inside Edward's cane. It reminded me of the stiletto heels I had seen before the murder but not since. The bottom of the one of those heels, it seemed to me, would be just the right size to create the hole in Rex's temple."

Kritzer's face did calisthenics. I could tell he didn't want to ask, but he had to. "You're telling me you know whose shoes these are?"

"Oh, yes. Her name is Olympia Fail. She went into the restroom shortly before you arrived."

Having no female officers handy, Kritzer fumed while bookstore owner Callista Jordache, Melanie Swann, cozy writer Pandora Wheatley, and a number of other women I didn't know came out of the restroom.

After about five agonizing minutes of pace-filled waiting, Kritzer said, "Are you sure this Quail woman is in there, McCabe?"

"Fail. Olympia Fail. I have not taken my eyes off the restroom door since she went in."

"Maybe she's done something fatal to herself," I suggested. "I don't think the woman's playing with a full deck."

"That's what their lawyers usually say," Kritzer informed us. "I'm not fond of that plea."

But after another five minutes that seemed like fifteen, and still lacking a female officer on the scene, Kritzer asked Lynda to go into the restroom and see if Fail was all right.

"What if she's armed?" I objected.

"She's wearing flats now, Jeff," Lynda threw over her shoulder as she moved toward the john.

A couple of minutes later she came out alone, wearing the dazed expression of a kid at a magic show who wonders where the rabbit came from—or, rather, where it went.

"I don't know what happened to her, but I swear the woman's not in there. She's vanished."

Chapter Twenty-Seven
A Fangirl's Curious Questions

Kritzer exploded. "That's nuts. That just can't be."

"I completely agree," Lynda said coldly. "But there's nobody in that ladies' room."

The Captain turned on Mac. "She came out. You just didn't see her. You must have taken your eyes off the restroom door at some point."

"I did not."

"Besides," I chipped in, "I was also watching because he was watching. We're not talking a long period of time between when she went in there and when you arrived on the scene, so it's not like we had to be on the alert for hours."

That was the point at which the razor-keen Cody sixth sense told me that Kritzer had begun to hate me as much as he hated his seventh-grade tormentor. I read the disgust on his face.

Kritzer instructed Lt. DeVore to have a female officer sent over. But the Lieutenant—an officious type who must have just made the Cincinnati Police Department's height requirement—pointed out that was unnecessary because Lynda had said the restroom was empty. He marched into the lavatory himself, with a sergeant posted outside.

"I'm going to take a flyer here and guess that you can tell me why this woman might have wanted to kill

Carter," Kritzer said. "Some kind of looney vendetta against mystery writers maybe?"

Not that theory again!

Although he'd addressed Mac, I answered.

"She's crazy, but not that crazy." I paused, and then corrected myself. "Well, actually she *is* that crazy. She was infuriated at Carter because he wrote a book killing off his roguish hero, of which she was apparently the world's greatest fan. The smart money says she killed him in revenge."

The Kritzer face was a study in perplexity. "Are you shitting me?"

"Sometimes fans get a little carried away."

"When Conan Doyle killed off Sherlock Holmes in 'The Final Problem,' one woman wrote a letter that began, 'You brute'," Mac recalled.

"But she didn't kill him," Lynda noted.

"I believe I used the word 'crazy' in reference to Ms. Fail," I said. This was no time to mention that I'd had bad vibes about Fail ever since lunch the day before, when she'd babbled on about soda leeching my bones. "The woman was obsessed with Ian St. George."

Suddenly I had a vision of how she'd killed Carter. And just for the record, I had it right. "There's a marble ledge in that alcove where we found the body. She must have set a book there for Carter to sign. When he bent over, she slipped off one of her shoes and drove the stiletto heel into his temple."

At this point the Lieutenant came out of the ladies' loo and shook his head—no Olympia Fail.

"What say you, Mr. Malvern?" Mac asked. "You seemed to know Ms. Fail better than anyone at QueenCon, from my observation."

I'd forgotten all about Paul Malvern, Carter's Boswell and recently Olympia Fail's companion. He'd never left.

No deer in the headlights ever looked more surprised at being addressed. Maybe he'd also forgotten that he was there. It took him a few moments to respond, during which Kritzer looked eager to hear what he had to say.

"I guess that works. I mean, it must have been something like that. And it must have been Olympia who did it, if it was her shoe that killed Rex and she took a powder when she saw that you were on to her."

"Of course," said Mac. "However, I was actually wondering whether you could support Jefferson's analysis of her motive. I always pay attention to motive."

Who, me? That was the expression on Malvern's face.

"I'd never met the woman until a little more than twenty-four hours ago at lunch," he protested. "She kind of latched on to me like a leech after that, obviously because I was writing the Carter book. She kept asking me questions about him."

"What kind of questions?" Kritzer wanted to know.

"Questions like, 'Did he have any children?' Knowing Rex, that wasn't impossible. But if he did he either didn't know it or wouldn't own up to it. 'Who was the real love of his life?' 'Who was Sally Kincaid in *Cat's-paw* based on?' 'Did he ever think about the women—'"

"What did you tell her about Sally Kincaid?" Mac interrupted.

"Not Carter's best female character," Lynda opined. "Too clingy."

"Rex swore that he never based a character on a real person except in *Murder, By George,*" Malvern said. "Until then, he pulled the characters out of his head. He told me he always got a kick out of readers who thought they knew who a character was 'in real life.'"

"Strange questions," Kritzer commented.

"At least she was consistent," Lynda said. "She asked Carter himself about the model for the woman in that book at the reception on Friday night. He said there was no model, that the character was pure fiction. I, uh, couldn't help overhearing."

Once a journalist . . .

"Frankly, I got real tired of the third degree real fast," Malvern said. "Every time she disappeared for a while, I hoped she'd find another host to attach herself to."

"When she wasn't around you, she was around Carter himself," I said. "I'm surprised she wasn't at the book signing yesterday, hanging on his every witticism. At the time I figured that she'd already had all of her first, second, and third editions signed, plus paperback editions and e-books, but now that I realize—"

"Are you sure?" Mac demanded.

"Sure of what?"

"That she wasn't at the author signing?"

"You mean you didn't notice? You notice everything. You not only see, you observe." Okay, I was pouring it on thick, but I don't often get the chance.

"I was inscribing books myself, Jefferson, giving my loyal readers the full attention they deserved."

"Oh. To answer your question: Yes, I'm positive. Lynda and I talked about it at the time. Does it make any difference?"

"It makes all the difference, old boy!"

Chapter Twenty-Eight
Dead End

"So how was your mystery weekend?" Aneliese "Popcorn" Pokorny, my irreplaceable assistant, asked when I came through the office door on Monday morning.

"Oh, you know—same old, same old."

"Boss, there was a murder!"

"That's what I mean—same old, same old. Actually, it was very relaxing being totally away from work except for the stream of phone calls, text messages, and e-mails about Lani Alvarez's police brutality accusation."

Mac, true to form, had refused to expound on his cryptic comment about Olympia Fail's non-appearance at her victim's book signing. The rest of us, meaning Capt. Kritzer and the world at large, were more concerned with her non-appearance anywhere else after her post-panel potty break.

Joe Ziebart of the *Cincinnati Sentinel* and Morris Kindle of the AP had reported Fail's vanishing act in the most purple prose possible. "Cincinnati police today are searching for a murder suspect who mysteriously disappeared under the watchful eye of mystery novelist Sebastian McCabe," Z informed his readers. "Police believe they know who killed mystery writer Rex Carter," Morrie wrote. "The only problem is that she walked into a hotel restroom on Sunday afternoon and has not been seen since." I expected them to keep milking that cow for at least another week. And I shuddered to think of the lengths to which they might have to go to keep the story on life support.

Both journalists had also reported that a second death at the QueenCon mystery conference had been determined to be an accident. The elderly mystery maestro (good old Morrie Kindle had actually written "maestro") Edward Seton had suffered a heart attack, hitting his head on a piece of furniture when he fell.

Popcorn handed me my morning mug of decaf and made herself comfortable in the chair in front of my desk, hugging her own java. "I've read every story I could find online. Now dish."

I did so, going heavy on the Carter–LeSourde–Seton triangle in consideration of my audience. Popcorn, who has been fifty years old for several years and dates Erin Police Chief Oscar Hummel, devours steamy romance novels in her off time.

"So what do you think?" she asked when I'd finished. "How did she do it?"

"Beats me. It's a magic trick. That's Mac's province. He made noises about having an angle, but then he went into his imitation of a clam. Meanwhile, I suppose we should earn our paychecks. What should I know that I don't know?"

"I didn't see the need to bother you with this over the weekend, but our legal counsel called on Friday afternoon with a heads up. She wanted you to know that negotiations have broken down with a blind student who claims we didn't make the appropriate accommodations under the Americans with Disabilities Act. He may sue."

"The fun never ends here at SBU. It was nice of Kelly to call, but I should have been told about that business before it got to lawyer level." This is what's called preaching to the choir. "I'm sure Ralph just forgot. He's had a tough month."[11]

Cody's Law: The best way to make sure a thing doesn't happen is to prepare for it. Some of my best work has been done getting ready for a media crisis that didn't break, but I don't begrudge a minute of it.

So I spent most of the morning getting ready to respond to inquiries about the disgruntled student. That involved calling Ralph Pendergast, our lame-duck provost, and Kelly Richards, the legal eagle. Ralph and I had never gotten on, but now that he was on his way out to greener pastures I missed him already. Ms. Richards is that *rara avis*, a lawyer who actually speaks English. Between the two of them I got a good handle on what had actually happened. Then I crafted talking points in case there was a lawsuit and (a) the student's lawyer called a news conference or otherwise alerted media to the filing, or (b) an overworked reporter actually had time to go trolling through the online filings for a suit that looked interesting.

"Where do we stand with Alvarez?" I asked Ms. Richards while I had her on the line.

"Once that young lady realizes she's gotten all the publicity she's going to get out of the brutality charge, I think we can resolve the issue with a fairly small cash payment and an apology from the officer and Father Joe."

"Sounds good."

Our president, the benign Father Joseph Pirelli, would sign the apology, but I would write it—and the one from the officer (her former sociological experiment) as well. I was already forming Father's Joe's words in my head as I hung up the phone: "On behalf of myself and the entire St. Benignus University community, I wish to express sincere regret that . . ."

---

[11] See *Erin Go Bloody*, MX Publishing, 2016.

Lynda interrupted my mind-work with a text: *"Still have job for now. No ex-royal hanging around office."* Call it gallows humor. The specter of a Grier takeover must have been haunting my beloved like the memory of a bad date. (Not that she and I ever had a bad date together, but she must have had some before me. I don't ask.) For the record, in case you don't read the *Wall Street Journal*, the Bonhaus–Grier dance went on for some time. I texted back: *"Don't give up your night job – the bourbon and horses novel."* When she sent back a thumbs-up sign, it seemed to me rather sad that our grandchildren would never have the joy of someday finding these tender love notes.

I'd just finished eating a salad at my desk for lunch when Mac strolled in, a look of extreme self-satisfaction on his hirsute face. He visits me in my work habitat a lot, but never without reason. Our offices are in different buildings and he doesn't walk just for exercise.

"What's up, my complacent-looking friend?" I asked.

"I have been chatting with Cal Daley in Public Safety. He still has strong connections at the Cincinnati police. They tell him that Ricky Kritzer was unable to find a trace of Olympia Fail."

"So what's news about that?"

"You misunderstand me. I mean that he was unable to find a trace of her *anywhere*—no Twitter account, no Facebook page, nothing like that. She paid her QueenCon registration by money order and used a Post Office Box that was rented only a month ago and paid for in the same manner. Also, she wiped her fingerprints from the murder shoe."

I'd assumed that murder by shoe would indicate a lack of premeditation, but apparently I'd assumed wrong. "So she must have planned all along to kill Carter and then disappear."

"Undoubtedly that is so. And yet, one could equally accurately say that Olympia Fail never disappeared at all."

He wanted me to respond with shock and amazement. Feeling contrary, I pulled the tab off a Caffeine-Free Diet Coke and gave it a guzzle. After a less-than-dramatic pause for me to say something, he gave up and continued.

"I have been examining certain birth records, Jefferson. You may recall that in 'The Adventure of the Noble Bachelor,' Sherlock Holmes concluded that Lady St. Simon did not disappear because Lady St. Simon never existed. In a similar way, Olympia Fail never existed. And yet I rather think that by this evening I shall be able to produce a photo of her."

Chapter Twenty-Nine
Caught

It isn't often that a small bookstore like Mo's Mysteries & Marvels in a small town like Erin hosts a whole bevy of published writers, even if they were mostly up-and-comers rather than established names. But the proximity of QueenCon XI to Erin had given Mo Russert (and her silent partner, Sebastian McCabe) a unique opportunity.

Thus it was that Monday, the day after Olympia Fail disappeared and the con ended, a sandwich-sign outside the former fire station on Water Street proclaimed: **BOOK SIGNING 8 P.M. TONIGHT – 6 AUTHORS!** In addition to Mac, the authors included Marcus Garber, Lisa Ballantine, Giles Hawthorne, Melanie Swann, and Augustus Fitch, who would sign cards promoting his Simon and Samantha Dale e-books.

At 5:30, all of the above were to be found at The Speakeasy, Erin's trendy gastropub, along with yours truly, Lynda, Kate, Paul Malvern, Alison LeSourde, Lafcadio Figg, Avis Tiffin, and Johanna Rawls. Mo, whom I'd expected to attend, was minding the store (which, coincidentally, had originally been located in the building that now housed The Speakeasy). We took up two large tables near each other on the recently opened patio. If the presence of LeSourde and Tall Rawls at one of them hasn't already tipped you off that something more than steak and salmon was on the evening's menu, then you're running behind me. I knew right away they weren't just there to fill out the table.

After the standard meaningless discussion about QueenCon over cocktails and dinner, the talk inevitably turned to the number one topic on everybody's mind—the murder of Rex Carter.

"I still can't believe that a fan would be wacko enough to kill a writer for doing away with a fictional character," Garber proclaimed. "Maybe we should all give up this writing gig for self-protection." I made a mental note to tell my romantic assistant the next day that he was holding his wife's hand, as a newlywed should. Popcorn would appreciate that detail.

"Oh, the slaying of Rex Carter was a crime much worse than mere murder," Mac announced almost cheerfully.

"What could be worse than murder?" LeSourde asked.

"Patricide."

The tables grew quiet.

"Father-killing," Malvern murmured—whether in surprise or as a public service to those with deficiencies in Latin I didn't know.

"The nature of the questions Olympia Fail asked you about Rex Carter—whether he had children, who was the model for one of his female characters—caught my attention," Mac told the biographer. "You essentially responded that either he was childless or he did not own up to any paternity. You referred, obviously, to his reputation as a womanizer. That reminded me that you, Ms. LeSourde, rather hedged your comment on that topic when you said, and I quote, 'at least I don't think Rex had any children.'"

"And Olympia Fail was young enough to be his daughter!" my wife said.

"Indeed, Lynda, you made that very observation on Friday night at the reception. You later reported overhearing Ms. Fail insist to Rex at that same event that a character in one of his books must have been based on a real woman. I strongly suspect she referred to her mother. She later asked Mr. Malvern about the same character."

Malvern nodded. "Sally Kincaid in *Cat's-paw*."

LeSourde, sitting next to Kate, looked shaken. "I can't believe it! I know what I said, but I never really dreamed that Rex . . ." She shook her head.

"Everything you've said is certainly very suggestive, Sebastian, so I won't niggle that it's not conclusive," Figg said. "I'm willing to believe that this Olympia Fail person was Rex Carter's unacknowledged and perhaps unknown daughter until she turns up and either admits it or proves the idea false. But why would she kill her father?"

"For his money," Giles Hawthorne suggested. "A claim on the estate, which she might—rightly or wrongly — assume was substantial."

"Most state laws do protect a child from being accidentally disinherited by a mistaken omission, but it's a little complicated," Augustus Fitch put in. He seemed proud to know this. "I researched that when I was writing *The Enigma of the Siamese Triplet*. Of course, she might also have simply assumed she could inherit."

Mac spread his hands. "Well, she might have assumed those things, true enough. However, she would then have to further assume that she could suddenly declare herself Rex's child without arousing suspicion, having failed to mention this before his death."

Nobody ever said that Olympia Fail had all of her screws on tight, Mac.

"No," he continued, "I think it far more likely that her patricidal act was fueled by the hatred felt by a young woman who acutely suffered the loss of a father's love throughout her life. The vicious method of the murder supports that. So does the fact that she killed him even though his natural death by cancer was widely known to be just weeks away, at best. She was driven not by revenge for the death of Ian St. George, not by greed for Rex Carter's estate, but by the animus of an abandoned child for whom the natural death of her hated father was not satisfactory. She wanted to be the agent of destruction herself. Perhaps she would call that ironic justice."

"That makes a kind of sense, I suppose," Melanie Swann said, "but I don't see where it's any more likely than the idea that she hacked him because she was irate that he killed off the Ian St. George character."

"I guess we won't know for sure until Fail gets caught," Lisa Ballantine said, "and I'm sure she will."

"I certainly hope so!" LeSourde said.

"I admit the disappearing act was pretty cute," the police procedural writer came back, "but it's hard to stay disappeared in the Internet age, when just about everything we do or say is recorded or photographed by somebody."

"As a matter of fact," Mac said mildly, "that has already happened." And that's when he pulled the rabbit out of his hat. Okay, he didn't have a hat and he actually held up a tablet computer, but you know what I mean.

"On this tablet I have a photo of a woman whom you may recognize as Olympia Fail." Technically speaking, as Mac pointed out to me later, that was not a lie.

Sensation! Almost everybody at our tables had something meaningless to say about the photo, which afforded a clear view of a tall woman in long, platinum hair parted in the middle and a white eyepatch on her left eye. She stood in full frontal view, paused on the steps of an impressive brick and stone building, as if caught by a security camera.

"Where was that taken?" Avis Tiffin asked.

"Would you believe New York?" Mac asked, another non-lie.

No, I wouldn't believe it—because I know the Public Library of Erin and Sussex County's main branch on Mulberry Street when I see it. What was Mac up to?

"There's something wrong about this, Mac," Lynda said. "She doesn't look quite right. Oh! I know—"

"Hold that thought, please!" Mac instructed. "Ms. Swann?"

"Yes." She seemed startled at being addressed.

"Did you encounter Ms. Fail during QueenCon?"

"I guess you could say that. I remember exchanging a few pleasantries with her at some point."

"And you remember what she looked like?"

"Yes. Certainly. With that eyepatch one wouldn't be likely to forget."

"No, we were not supposed to forget. That was the point of the eyepatch. Now, do you see anything different about Olympia Fail in this photograph compared to the woman that you saw and spoke to?"

She shook her head. "No, I don't, Mr. McCabe. She looks exactly the way I remember her. What are you getting at?"

I saw it then, finally—way behind Lynda on that one. So that's why Tall Rawls was there!

"You should see something different, Ms. Swann, but I can understand why you of all people would not."

"What are you talking about?" Fitch snapped.

"It's the eyepatch!" Malvern burst out. "I get it now—the eyepatch is on the wrong side."

"That's what I was trying to say before you cut me off, Mac," Lynda complained.

Mac nodded. "Brava, Lynda. You not only saw but observed, as the good journalist you are. And of course you would notice the change, Mr. Malvern, having spent some time in conversation over the weekend with the woman you knew as Olympia Fail. This experiment was not intended to fool you."

"Experiment?" Malvern echoed. *Right, as in "mad scientist."*

"Perhaps 'test' would be a better word. Earlier today, at my request, Ms. Rawls here donned a platinum blonde wig and an eyepatch to transform herself into a semblance of Olympia Fail for purpose of that photograph. I asked her to put the eyepatch on her left eye, not on the right as worn by the missing Ms. Fail. I felt certain that you would not detect the difference, Ms. Swann."

Melanie Swann looked annoyed. "What's your point?"

"The point is that the positioning of the eyepatch on the face in the photograph looked right to you *because you were used to seeing a reverse image in the mirror when you assumed the identity of Olympia Fail.*"

Chapter Thirty
From the Mind of a Mystery Writer

Melanie Swann played it just right, I'll give her that—equal parts astonishment and outrage.

"What are you saying? Are you nuts?"

Sebastian McCabe, never lacking in the self-confidence department, sailed on.

"I admire your equanimity when presented with a photo of a woman you knew did not exist. You must have thought the resemblance was a gift from heaven that had thrown law enforcement off the track. For myself, by contrast, I have no plaudits. I was a fool not to realize sooner that Olympia Fail was nothing more than a wig, an eyepatch, and a pair of impossibly high heels to make the wearer look taller as well as provide a murder weapon."

Lynda poked me in a rib. "I told you that hair was a wig."

Mac ignored the interruption.

"This woman who was supposed to be the world's greatest Ian St. George fangirl wore an eyepatch just as he did—but white instead of black. It was as if she were paradoxically proclaiming herself to the world as the anti-St. George. There was a practical advantage of the eyepatch as well: It kept anyone from looking at her face too closely for fear being thought rude and insensitive. Surely, however, its primary function was that of disguise, as was her rather thick Southern accent."

"You're going to be embarrassed when that woman shows up somewhere south of the Mason–Dixon line," Swann said.

"That is what is technically known as a 'bluff,' Ms. Swann, and a short-term one. You well know that Olympia Fail never existed, which is why the Cincinnati Police Department has been unable to find any traces of her, digital or otherwise. The question then becomes, 'Who was she really?'

"Jefferson noted that Olympia Fail, the obsessive Carter–St. George devotee, was not in line to get the author's inscription on a book during the author signing on Saturday. Why not? Surely this was not an event she would have passed up no matter how many inscribed books of his she already owned. I concluded that an appearance by Olympia Fail must have been impossible because she was already there under another persona—her true identity—as one of the other mystery writers signing books. One of the women, to be precise. I would not automatically rule out a man in theory, but as a practical matter none of the male authors present at the signing could have been transformed into Ms. Fail even in my rather robust imagination."

He didn't have to spell it out: Marcus Garber was too burly, Giles Hawthorne too pudgy, and Augustus Fitch too old.

"So I considered the women. Ms. Ballantine, in addition to being well alibied, is much too short even with those deadly four-inch high heels. And would a blonde disguise herself with a platinum blonde wig, even if there were a symbolism attached? Not likely. I ruled her out."

"Whew," Ballantine said. As comic relief, that was weak stuff.

"Melanie Swann, on the other hand, has short, dark hair. Although only medium in height when she wore flats, those stiletto heels of Olympia Fail would give the illusion of being a six-footer. She also wears glasses, which might explain why Ms. Fail on several occasions didn't seem to see very well."

"I would think a bad eye that had to be covered with an eyepatch would explain that to the satisfaction of most people," Swann said coolly.

"What about their body shapes?" Lynda said.

"Ms. Swann appears bulkier than her alter ego, I grant you." *Look who's talking!* "Most likely at one time she was somewhat larger before losing weight to pull off this charade. However, I am confident that under that loose sweater that she is wearing even today you will find several other layers of bulk-supplying clothing. Disprove that if you can, Ms. Swann."

She snorted. "I don't have to play your silly game. This whole idea that somebody could adopt a disguise and fool people close-up is just nuts."

Mac lifted an eyebrow. "I am surprised that you of all people would say so, Ms. Swann. Disguise figures in a number of your books. It is one of the romantic elements that distinguish them from most of your competitors on the hard-boiled side of the house.

"Of course, disguising yourself as a person that you created is a much different proposition from impersonating a real person to someone who knows that person, which truly would be almost impossible."

"Except for twins," Avis Tiffin stuck in.

"Indeed. Note that Olympia Fail had not just one or two characteristics that set her apart from others and drew our attention, but a whole host of them. Consider her Southern accent and how far removed it was from Melanie Swann's flat Midwestern speech patterns. I suspect that if I took the effort to find copies of her high school yearbooks I would find that she was engaged in theatrics during that period of her life—perhaps something along the lines of *Steel Magnolias*."

Direct hit! That's what the expression on Swann's face told me.

"Presumably the idea was to create a fall guy for the murder," Figg said. *Shouldn't that be "fall gal"?* "But it all seems so baroque, so overly complicated."

"Indeed," Mac agreed. "Only a mystery writer, and one of Ms. Swann's ilk, would think of such a thing. And, having created this mythical mystery fan, to make her disappear into thin air in true Golden Age fashion was icing on the cake. Unlike a true artist, however, she did not know where to stop. She gave us too much icing and too much cake."

"Enough with the metaphors," Lynda said, snatching the words right out of my brain. "The vanishing act was pretty simple, really, if Olympia Fail and Melanie Swann are the same person. I saw Melanie come out of that bathroom."

Mac sighed. "Alas, all magic tricks, like all Sherlockian deductions, are transparent once they are explained. Olympia Fail dematerialized forever with the removal of a wig, an eye-patch, and her clothing in a restroom stall—all of which were carried out of the room in the notably capacious handbag Ms. Swann carried with her all weekend. She has it with her even now."

"Wait a minute." Lisa Ballantine made a "time out" gesture. "Where was that big handbag when she went into the john?"

"In the inexpensive QueenCon tote bag, AKA 'swag bag,' given to every participant. Although it was much smaller than the handbag, the latter was canvas and easily folded up. When Ms. Swann exited the restroom, the tote went into her handbag along with everything that constituted Olympia Fail."

"Awesome," Avis Tiffin breathed. "Obviously, she didn't count on you being there to figure it all out, Mr. McCabe."

Swann shot the QueenCon volunteer a venomous look before regaining control, putting her face muscles back in neutral.

"*Au contraire*," Mac said. "I think I was part of her plan from the beginning, or very nearly so. When she sat next to us in her Fail persona during the luncheon on Saturday she commented on my minor reputation as an amateur sleuth. I believe that she deliberately left a trail of clues like breadcrumbs leading to Olympia Fail, a woman so obsessed with the character of Ian St. George that I was to believe she killed his creator in revenge for his demise. I apologize, Ms. Swann, for being so slow to catch on to the murder weapon that you had to call the police and tell them where to find it. We know the tipster was a woman, and I believe that you were that woman."

Swann rewarded this assertion with a tight smile. "Well, I must say this is certainly the most unusual pre-signing dinner I've ever been to."

"What you said about Olympia Fail being Rex's daughter—that applied to this woman?" Alison LeSourde nodded toward Swann, who I suppose would have been her stepdaughter.

"Precisely. In her appearance on the private eye panel on Saturday morning, she implied that her father and mother were only slightly acquainted." I remembered that: *Oh, yes. He wrote my mother a note to tell her it was nice meeting her. She never saw him again, but she kept that note until the day she died.* "From Ms. Swann's Wikipedia entry, I knew that she was born in St. Louis and the date. It was a simple matter to look up her birth certificate online using a genealogy site that has been helpful to me in tracing my own family, although records on Clan McCabe are regrettably scanty prior to the fourteenth century. Surely, Ms. Swann, you are aware that the name listed on your birth certificate under 'father' is Rex Carter."

She considered playing dumb, if I read her face right, but gave that up as a bad job.

"Okay, you win. He was my father. But I didn't want anybody to know that while he was alive and his death didn't change anything. I wanted to make it as a mystery writer on my own, not as the daughter of somebody relatively famous in the field. My mother never asked for child support, so why should I get any benefit out of being his daughter? That's just an insignificant biological fact."

As speeches go, I gave her an "A-minus" for content but a "C" for delivery because she tried to project an emotional detachment that was far from real. And then came the part that I totally believed:

"My mother called out his name right before she died. I told him that last year at Magna cum Murder, where we were both on panels. He claimed he didn't even remember her. But that couldn't be true, it just couldn't."

"Because you felt sure that the strong female character in *Cat's-paw* must have been based on her," Mac said.

She shook her head. "No, I didn't think of that when I read the book. But this Olympia Fail person might have been on to something about that."

"So you still deny being Fail?" Tall Rawls asked, stepping out of her observer-only role.

"Of course. The idea is absurd. The mirror image ploy was very cute, but it hardly proves anything." Melanie Swann picked up her handbag and opened it up. "See—no wig, no eyepatch."

Mac looked pained. "I am quite sure those elements of disguise, as well as the Fail wardrobe, have been safely discarded in some anonymous trash can somewhere between Cincinnati and Erin."

Swann stood up, lifting the handbag over her shoulder. "If I were writing this as a mystery, I would make sure my sleuth could build a case that would actually stand up in court. You're not anywhere near that, McCabe. All you have is a nice chain of reasoning that falls laughably short of proof. I presume I'm supposed to confess based on that. Sorry to disappoint you. You never caught the killer in the Phillimore case, did you? I guess this is a kind of reprise."

Chapter Thirty-One
Proof

"But you knew the identity of Phillimore's killer," Kate said after Swann had walked out the door. "You just never brought him to justice."

"Precisely the point of Ms. Swann's taunt, my dear," Mac said grimly.

"So, no story for me," Tall Rawls said.

"That happy outcome has been delayed, not derailed, Johanna, and through no fault of yours. Your impersonation of Olympia Fail worked up to a point, even though you are really too tall for the part. Ms. Swann fell into my mirror-image trap. However, I underestimated her ability to maintain composure in the face of the unexpected. I thought that she would, if not confess, at least be shocked into saying something indiscreet."

"And I'm so surprised she didn't," Lisa Ballantine said with almost Cody-esque sarcasm. "Stunts like that always work in Golden Age mysteries."

Her husband of three days, the creator of chef and amateur sleuth Pierre LeGrande, started to open his mouth but thought better of it.

"Well, Sebastian, this is hardly the outcome I had hoped for," Figg said, the expression on his face belying his words.

"Your disappointment and surprise can only be a pale reflection of my own, I assure you, Lafcadio."

But the biggest surprise of the evening awaited us at Mo's Mysteries & Marvels. Melanie Swann showed up to sign books.

"I can't believe it," Lynda muttered as we stood in a corner of the former fire station, watching the patricidal maniac glad-hand readers.

"Her picture should be in the dictionary under 'chutzpah,'" I agreed.

I've been to book signings where authors gave talks, some of which were nothing more than commercials, followed by the chance to buy a book and have it inscribed. But with so many authors at Mo's event, it was more like a meet and greet with cookies and punch. Stacks of books by the visiting authors were laid out on one table in the middle of the room, with the refreshments on another.

Bright-eyed and dark haired Mo Russert, having no clue that Melanie Swann's plotting wasn't confined to the printed page, introduced everybody with her normal enthusiasm while Mac scowled.

"It's a rare treat here at Mo's Mysteries & Marvels to host some of the best and brightest mystery writers working today," the bookstore's eponymous co-owner effused. *Not to mention a killer, Mo, but you don't know that.*

The audience of maybe three dozen book lovers included Oscar Hummel, police chief and failed mystery writer (he couldn't solve the mystery he set up, so he never finished his inaugural novel); Popcorn, his main squeeze and my right arm at the office; Sister Mary Margaret Malone, Lynda's best friend; and most members of the Poisoned Pens, our local mystery writers' group.

Except for Swann, the writers who were there to sign books still looked shaken by the curtain-raiser at The Roundhouse. Most managed a nod or wave as their names were mentioned. But "the author of the amazing Birdy Edwards historical mysteries" smiled in our direction.

"In theory, making the case against her may not be as difficult as it seems at this juncture," Mac told us. "Forensic analysis will establish that those stiletto heels killed Rex Carter. We have multiple witnesses to tie those shoes to Olympia Fail, thereby forging a strong link in the chain of circumstantial evidence to prove her guilt in the murder. We can also show the connection between Melanie Swann and Carter. What we need is a way to prove that Ms. Fail and Ms. Swann are the same person, tying it all together."

I thought about that. *One person, two names . . . two hotel rooms!*

"Maybe." I stopped. "No, never mind. That kind of things only works on *Columbo*."

"I love that old show," Lynda said. "'Just one more thing, ma'am!'"

"Come on, old boy, speak now or forever hold your peace," Mac urged me. "A preposterous notion is better than none at all."

Not sure whether to be complimented or insulted, I spilled it: "I was just thinking that Swann must have rented a room under the Fail identity as well as her own name, right? If we could somehow link her to that room, it would be a nail in her coffin—especially since she claimed in front of witnesses that she didn't know Fail very well."

"Fingerprints!" Lynda said.

"I don't think a mystery writer, particularly one as devious as Melanie Swann, would make such an obvious mistake," I said. "That would be almost as bad as forgetting to wipe the murder weapon. But what if she got confused and turned in the wrong room key when she checked out as Swann?"

Mac raised both eyebrows. "By thunder, Jefferson, the idea has possibilities! Of course, it would be the sheerest chance, but no crime is ever solved without some measure of good fortune. Even Captain Baxter in Ms. Ballantine's police procedurals is the beneficiary of the occasional helpful coincidence."

He pulled out his smartphone and left the room.

"What do you think he's doing?" Lynda asked.

"Calling somebody." Mac always knows somebody who knows somebody.

Lynda rolled her eyes. "Tell me something I don't know. I was wondering who specifically he's calling. Hey, don't you want to buy some of Melanie's books? You seemed to enjoy *The End of the Line*."

"I did. But I hate it in retrospect."

"I'm going to try one of those Chef LeGrande books. Marcus Garber seems like a decent sort."

"You might want to start with *Cream of the Crime*—that's the first."

Shortly after she came back with that very book, its cover colorfully illustrated with a humorous drawing of the murder victim drowning in whipped cream, Mac also returned.

"Well?" I said.

"Alas, the longshot did not pay off, if I may couch a metaphor in the argot of the gambling community. With some difficulty I reached Bill Crane, the chief of security at the Fountain Square Hotel. He informed me that the plastic passes which we anachronistically call keys are demagnetized almost as soon as they are returned to the desk. Therefore, even if Ms. Swann turned in the wrong key, there is no way to know that."

"So we're sunk," Lynda said.

"Let us say, rather, that we are still looking for a life boat. I still have hope, and hope does not disappoint."

As if she'd heard him, Melanie Swann looked up from signing a book and once again smiled in our direction.

I was about halfway through my granola the next morning when my smartphone burst out in "You're So Vain," my ringtone for Sebastian McCabe.

"Cody & Cody Detective Agency," I said. "We solve mysteries, puzzles, riddles, enigmas, conundrums, posers, and—"

"Ah, Jefferson! I am pleased to find you in so ebullient a mood at this early hour. Your mood matches my own. I will pick you up in approximately five minutes."

"I suppose it would be rude to ask where we are going." But I was speaking to a dial tone.

"What was that all about?" Lynda asked over her cup of caffeine-au-lait.

"I'm not sure, but I think it was a call to hounds."

After quickly finishing my breakfast and brushing my teeth, I made one more stop. On a hunch, I rooted through my bag of detritus from QueenCon and picked up a two-inch by three-and-a-half-inch piece of cardboard that had been handed to me on Saturday.

"Text me," Lynda called as I flew out the door in response to a blow from Mac's obnoxious horn. I was surprised to find that the front seat of his obscenely large, fire-engine red 1959 Chevy was already occupied.

"Good morning," said Tall Rawls. "Looks like I'm going to get a story after all."

"Congratulations. Maybe you even know where we're going."

"The airport," Mac said as I climbed in the back seat. "Did I forget to mention that?"

"Why are we going there?"

"The first flight to St. Louis leaves at nine-oh-five. It is my hope that we can speak with Ms. Swann before she enters the terminal. Ricky—that is, Captain Kritzer—has agreed to meet us at the curbside check-in location."

"You got Kritzer to play along? You *are* a magician."

"I would not claim that the Captain has any greater confidence in me than in the past, much less affection, but Bill Crane is a good friend of his from the latter's days on the force."

"Okay, I'm missing something here, because the last I heard my brilliant idea about the hotel key didn't pan out."

"Indeed it did not. That led to a sleepless night for me until I realized there could be another way to tie Ms. Swann to the hotel room she rented under the Olympia Fail nom-de-homicide, to coin a neologism."

And then he explained.

I mentally smacked myself in the head. "But that's so obvious. How come it took you all night to think of it? Some genius you are!"

"You guys crack me up," Johanna said.

"I suppose I should also mention that Ricky extorted from me a promise to keep my mouth shut as he confronts Ms. Swann."

"Direct quote?"

"Not exactly, Jefferson. He also employed a colorful but inaccurate description for my facial orifice. I can but console myself with the proverbial assurance that silence is golden."

Don't expect to see Captain Kritzer pounding down beers in the McCabe man cave any time soon, but he has no legitimate beef about the way Mac held up his end of the bargain that morning.

It is a curious fact, and the source of endless amusement to big-city sophisticates, that the Cincinnati airport is in Kentucky. This makes more sense when you know that it is actually the Cincinnati/Northern Kentucky International Airport. Erin, like the Queen City, sits just across the river from Kentucky. We crossed it on the ferry that goes back and forth all day long.

When we pulled up to the curbside check-in outside the Delta Terminal, I could see Kritzer pacing. A slightly shorter black man, Bill Crane, sipped coffee from a White Castle cup.

"Good morning, gentlemen," Mac boomed.

"That's the last thing you're going to say," Kritzer told him. His tie hung slightly crooked around his thick neck.

Mac didn't respond, thereby following the order.

Tall Rawls pulled out her reporter's notebook. "How do you spell your last name, Captain?"

Swann showed up about twenty-five minutes later. I spotted her first getting out of a cab. She wore a yellow blouse that made her look much less padded than the Velma sweater. I pointed her out to Kritzer. Without a word he marched quickly her way, the rest of us trailing in his wake.

"Ms. Swann!"

She handed a tip to the cab driver and looked around.

"I'm Captain Richard Kritzer from the Cincinnati Police Department homicide unit."

"I remember you. We talked briefly at the hotel on Sunday."

She pretended the rest of us weren't there.

"Yes, ma'am. You were one of the women who left the ladies' room after Olympia Fail, the suspect in the Rex Carter homicide, had entered."

"Did you find her?"

"I think we did and I think we have a pretty good case against her. The coroner says the heel of that bloody shoe we found fits the fatal wound on Mr. Carter's temple. We have not only witnesses, but numerous photos shot with cell phones that establish Ms. Fail as the person wearing those shoes."

Melanie Swann looked at her watch. "I have a plane to catch, Lieutenant."

You're thinking of Columbo.

"Captain." He gave her a look that would have made me confess even if I hadn't done anything wrong. His eyes looked more steel than hazel. "So that's the beginning of a case against Olympia Fail and I'm sure we can flesh it out. By the way, this is Bill Crane, director of security for the Fountain Square Hotel."

Crane nodded, but didn't say it was a pleasure to meet her.

"I asked Bill to examine the video from the security cameras on the sixth floor, where Fail's room was located. They show you on several occasions entering the room in what I would call a furtive manner, looking both ways first, and her coming out. And also vice versa—Fail going into that room and you coming out."

So that had been Mac's brainstorm! And why hadn't I thought of it? The security video on the guest floors had already come into play earlier in establishing that no one had entered Ned Seton's room the morning he died.

"A reasonable person would have to conclude that Melanie Swann and Olympia Fail are one and the same person," Kritzer concluded. "You kept the room under the Fail name so that you could be seen coming out of it and mingle with other conventioneers in the elevator in a memorable way, adding to the illusion of Olympia Fail."

"That's bogus. You made it up, that stuff about the video."

"Not this time, Melanie." Jeff Cody hadn't promised Kritzer to keep my blanking mouth shut.

"There are no fingerprints on the shoe, of course," the Captain droned on, "but a DNA swab will eventually prove that you wore it, Ms. Swann."

I handed her the piece of cardboard that I had thought to bring from home at the last minute that morning. She stared at it. "What the hell is this?"

"Aristotle O'Doul's business card. I'm sure he'd like you to give him a call."

A Few Words of Thanks

Once again Jeff Cody and Dan Andriacco both need to thank all the people whose talented work helped to made this latest Sebastian McCabe–Jeff Cody adventure see the light of day:

Ann Brauer Andriacco, for her constant assistance and encouragement, as well as her readership;

Deacon Royce Winters, retired Cincinnati police officer, for his insights on procedures in homicide cases in the Queen City;

Ron Gustafson, for his experience in dealing with the deaths of guests during his career as a hotel manager;

Bob Byrne, for reminding me of murder methods in Nero Wolfe stories and Kieran McMullen for helping me create the murder method in this one;

Jeff Suess, for proofreading and final preparation of the manuscript; and

Steve Winter, yet again, for giving the manuscript the incredible benefit of his engineering eye.

Special thanks, as always, must go to Steve Emecz for being the world's most easy-to-work-with publisher and to Brian Belanger for an outstanding cover.

About the Author

Dan Andriacco has been reading mysteries since he discovered Sherlock Holmes at the age of nine, and writing them almost as long. The first seven books in his popular Sebastian McCabe–Jeff Cody series are *No Police Like Holmes*, *Holmes Sweet Holmes*, *The 1895 Murder*, *The Disappearance of Mr. James Phillimore*, *Rogues Gallery*, *Bookmarked for Murder*, and *Erin Go Bloody*. He is also the co-author, with Kieran McMullen, of *The Amateur Executioner*, *The Poisoned Penman*, and *The Egyptian Curse* mysteries solved by Enoch Hale with Sherlock Holmes.

A member of the Tankerville Club, the Illustrious Clients, the Vatican Cameos, and an associate member of the Diogenes Club of Washington, D.C., Dan is also the author of *Baker Street Beat: An Eclectic Collection of Sherlockian Scribblings*. Follow his blog at www.danandriacco.com, his tweets at *@DanAndriacco*, and his Facebook Fan Page at: www.facebook.com/DanAndriaccoMysteries.

Dr. Dan and his wife, Ann, have three grown children and six grandchildren. They live in Cincinnati, Ohio, USA, about forty miles downriver from Erin.

Praise for the earlier
Sebastian McCabe–Jeff Cody mysteries

"This (*Erin Go Bloody*) is Dan Andriacco's best book to date! I feel I could actually walk around downtown Erin, Ohio and not get lost. The characters are charming and believable. These are always entertaining reads! I have become a huge fan of Mac, and Jeff!"
　　　　—Retired Sheriff Kenneth Ramsey, Sr.

"The ingenious twist at the end is an example of Andriacco's masterful ability to pen a page-turner. *Bookmarked for Murder* is a must-read for anyone who loves a classic who-done-it."
　　　　—Mystery writer Kathleen Kaska

"You're in the hands of a master of mystery plotting here. *Rogues Gallery* is a delightful read, hard to put down, and highly recommended. And did I say fun?"
　　　　—Hollywood screenwriter Bonnie MacBird

"The villain is hard to discern and the motives involved are even more obscure. All-in-all, this (*The Disappearance of Mr. James Phillimore*) is a fun read in a series that keeps getting better with each new tale."
　　　　—Philip K. Jones

"*The* 1895 *Murder* is the most smoothly-plotted and written Cody/McCabe mystery yet. Mr. Andriacco plays fair with the reader, but his clues are deftly hidden, much as Sebastian McCabe hides the secrets to his magic tricks under an entertaining run of palaver."
　　　　—*The Well-Read Sherlockian*

"I loved Dan Andriacco's first novel about Sebastian McCabe and Jeff Cody, and I'm delighted to recommend (*Holmes Sweet Holmes*), which has a curiously topical touch."
—Roger Johnson, *Sherlock Holmes Society of London*

"*No Police Like Holmes* is a chocolate bar of a novel—delicious, addictive, and leaves a craving for more."
—*Girl Meets Sherlock*

Also from MX Publishing

Visit www.mxpublishing.com for dozens of other Sherlock Holmes novels, novellas, short story collections, Conan Doyle biographies, Holmes travel books, and more.

MX Publishing is the award-winning, world's largest independent Sherlock Holmes Book publishers with over 100 new authors and 250 new Sherlock Holmes stories in print.